Thomas Cross

The Autobiography of a Stage-Coachman

Vol. I

Thomas Cross

The Autobiography of a Stage-Coachman
Vol. I

ISBN/EAN: 9783337013653

Printed in Europe, USA, Canada, Australia, Japan

Cover: Foto ©Raphael Reischuk / pixelio.de

More available books at **www.hansebooks.com**

THE AUTOBIOGRAPHY OF A STAGE-COACHMAN.

BY

THOMAS CROSS.

IN THREE VOLUMES.

VOL. I.

LONDON:
HURST AND BLACKETT, PUBLISHERS,
SUCCESSORS TO HENRY COLBURN,
13, GREAT MARLBOROUGH STREET.
1861.

LONDON:
PRINTED BY R. BORN, GLOUCESTER STREET,
REGENT'S PARK.

TO

HENRY VILLEBOIS, ESQ.,

THESE PAGES

ARE,

BY PERMISSION,

MOST RESPECTFULLY

AND GRATEFULLY DEDICATED

BY

THE AUTHOR.

PREFACE.

If in the perusal of this narrative it should be objected that there is far too much of a personal or private nature, the author's excuse is, that it was commenced to gratify a large circle, beyond whose limits it was never intended to pass; but some friends, thinking it worthy of a more extended circulation, have induced him to offer it to the public.

If it should be found not altogether to correspond with the title, and here and there to treat of persons and things in a manner not warranted by the position of the author, he claims the privilege of free agency, and shelters himself under the shadow of precedent.

In the Autobiography of a Stage-Coachman the reader must not expect to find any exalted sentiment, any imaginary tale, any burlesque review, or any very deep pathos; discursive as it may be, no caricature of everyday life, no pungent satire on the follies or fashions of the day, enlivens its pages—they contain merely a plain, unsophisticated detail of incidents and occurrences that came under the observation of a man who had daily intercourse with all classes of people.

CONTENTS OF VOL. I.

CHAPTER I.

A Novel Commencement—A London Coach-office—A Country one—A Provincial Book-keeper—Lord Bacon—Shakespere—Lord Byron—Inquisitiveness—An Important Confession—A Father—A Mother—A Prognostic—Alexander Pope—The Itchen—A Scene in Hampshire—Gibbon—A Popular Divine—A Tyrannical Pedagogue—An Instructor of Youth—A Long Ride—A Hasty Decision 1

CHAPTER II.

The Departure and Outfit—A Fourth-rate Man-of-War—Captain, Officers, and Crew—Sea-sickness—The Quarter-deck—The Cock-pit—An Accident—Lubber's Hole—The Schoolmaster—Midshipmen—Rio de Janeiro—An Extraordinary Feat—A False Alarm—The Captain's Table—A Court-martial, Sentence, and Execution—Scenes in the Gun-room and in the Captain's Cabin—A Pleasant Time—The Middle Watch—Fore and Afternoon Watches—The First Lieutenant—Corporal Punishment—The Haven 31

CHAPTER III.

Day-Dreams—The Shark and the Dolphin—Yarns—A Hard Hit—The Armourer's Chest—Calcutta—The Marquis Wellesley—The Return—Madras—A Scene in the Water—Trincomalee and Colombo—Bombay and Elephanta—The Straits of Sumatra, and the Captain's Advice—China Seas—A Typhoon—Canton—A Distinguished Naval Officer—Parting—An Historical Comparison—An Agreeable Shipmate—St. Helena—The Chops of the Channel—The Pilot Boat—A Polite Request—The Landing—Sentiment 74

CHAPTER IV.

A Coach Proprietor—Members of Parliament—A Welcome—Nelson's Funeral—The Theatres—George Frederick Cooke—John Kemble and Mrs. Siddons—The Country—A Death-bed Scene—An Elegy—The Lawyer—A Second Blow—The Wine Merchant—A Third Blow—A Valetudinarian—The Postmaster—A Scene at the Dinner-table—A Consultation and Trial—Unexpected Result—Philanthropy 110

CHAPTER V.

Convalescence—Thoughts for the Future—The Sixth Mate—Amusements—A Rash Adventure—A Literary Society—Junius—Lord Macaulay—A Character—A Fire—Gunpowder Companionship—Lord Gambier—Sir Eliab Harvey—Sir Roger Curtis—Lord Cochrane—A Curious Rencontre—The Prince of Wales—A Dreadful Explosion—Wonderful Escape—A Rash Attempt . 140

CHAPTER VI.

Younger Sister—Pleasant Gallop—Younger Brother—Pleasant Swim—Dreadful Disaster at Sea—A Naval Ball—Self-confidence—Domestic Sorrow—New Branch of an Old Acquaintance—Career of an Officer—A Distressed Mother, her Trials and her Death—Pleasant Life—A Welcome Visitor—Sad Calamity—A Trio—Duel—Pleasant Body Companion—The Comets of 1858 and of 1811—Description of—Astronomers 184

CHAPTER VII.

The New Forest—The Confines of Dorset—A Country Town—Shooting—Lord Chancellor Eldon—Encombe—Sir Walter Raleigh—Smoking—Lulworth—Corfe Castle—Edward the Martyr—King John—Lady Bankes—The Heroes of the Parliamentary Army—Christian Preachers—Education—An Original Sect—A Legend—The Isle of Wight—The Royal Cockpit—A Joke—The Duke of Devonshire—Two Foreign Princes—A Prince of Coach Proprietors—Friend in Need—A False Step—An Establishment—Wedding—Breach of the Law—Mr. Justice Burroughs—Soberton Downs—An Israelite Sportsman—A Bet—A Fracas—Law-Suit—Judge Gazelee—A Dispute on a Point of Law—Mr. Serjeant Pell . 230

CHAPTER VIII.

The War—Trafalgar—Sir John Moore—Sir David Baird—Corunna—Disembarkation—Walcheren—Camp at Southsea—Embarkation—The Earl of Chatham—Sir Richard John Strachan—Prosperity of Seaport Towns—A Profitable Business—A Distinguished Military Gentleman; his Wants Supplied—A Dinner and Wine—The Bill—An Interesting Discovery—Drive to Reading and Oxford—An Agreeable Surprise—Prompt Resolve—Clouds in the Distance—The Russian Campaign—The Campaign in Germany—Peace—The Visit to Portsmouth—Insanity of the People—Prince Blucher—The Emperor Alexander—The King of Prussia—Napoleon 277

THE AUTOBIOGRAPHY OF A STAGE-COACHMAN.

CHAPTER I.

BIRTH, PARENTAGE, AND EDUCATION.

A Novel Commencement—A London Coach-office—A Country one—A Provincial Book-keeper—Lord Bacon—Shakespere—Lord Byron—Inquisitiveness—An Important Confession—A Father—A Mother—A Prognostic—Alexander Pope—The Itchen—A Scene in Hampshire—Gibbon—A Popular Divine—A Tyrannical Pedagogue—An Instructor of Youth—A Long Ride—A Hasty Decision.

BEFORE the new method of travelling had quite superseded the old, when railways had not become so general as they now are, the establishment of the main or trunk lines had dispossessed those men of their seats whose names were as familiar as household words, when associated with the requirements, the business, and the pleasures of the community; and had driven them, like the ancient Britons, to the mountainous districts of Wales and Cornwall, or to the swamps and fens of the opposite side of our island, to follow their vocation, and to seek their subsistence.

It was then the fate of the author of this narrative to be engaged in driving a coach from one of the seaports on the eastern coast, where the enemy had not yet penetrated, but to which he bid fair soon to be a welcome visitor.

One cold, dark winter morning, a little before day, in the last decade of the first half of this present nineteenth century (my memory will not serve to state the precise year), I was walking leisurely from my lodgings, with my great-coat over my left arm, and my four-horse whip in my right hand, to the inn from which the coach daily took its departure.

On that particular morning some serious thoughts had arisen in my mind; and a hasty retrospect of my early days, contrasting strongly with the gloomy prospect before me, passed through my brain.

In London, the half-hour preceding the starting of perhaps five or six coaches from any of the large establishments, was a time of some little excitement. The neat and elegant Telegraph Coach, with its polished boot, on the hinder part of which was inscribed, in large characters, "The Times," "The Independent," "The Wonder," or some such appropriate name; the highly-varnished body, the blazing Golden Cross or the Spread Eagle conspicuous on the door panels; the motley crowd of people, of both sexes and all ranks, from the peer to the humble mechanic, some anxious to take their seats in or on these delightful conveyances; the well-groomed cattle, with their attendant horsekeeper, the harness all in the nicest order; the quantity of packages issuing from the booking-office; the instructions, not unmixed with a little good-natured banter, vulgarly called chaff, given by the book-keeper to the well-known characters about to proceed to their accustomed destination, formed altogether a scene not unworthy the pen or pencil of a Hogarth.

How different the same half-hour in a provincial town in one corner of the kingdom. On approaching the inn not a solitary person did I see. The dingy, half-washed coach stood by itself outside the gates, like a deserted ship; inside the yard there was a dim, dirty place set aside for the office; in it glimmered one poor mutton candle, stuck on a piece of rusty tin, that had served the ostler for a candlestick for years; by its light I entered, and could just perceive a lantern-jawed, melancholy-looking man, whose visage indicated—indeed, seemed already to anticipate—the fate that awaited both him and me, leaning with his head upon his hand, inert and heedless, as most men are who have nothing to do—this was the porter. On the other side of the counter, behind an old worm-eaten desk, sat the book-keeper. The usual salutation having passed between us, I took from the desk a long sheet of white paper, which, with the exception of the heading, was unsullied—not the name of a passenger or parcel was written thereon! This was what is technically called the "way-bill." With a complacency I could sometimes assume, I read the date aloud, adding thereto that it was a most remarkable day.

"Remarkable, Mr. C——, for what?" said my inquisitive friend, the book-keeper.

"Remarkable, Mr. B——," I repeated, "for its being the natal day, or, more properly speaking, the anniversary of the birth of three celebrated men."

"Indeed! Pray, who were they?"

"Why, Mr. B——," I said, "the first was a man of most profound wisdom and learning—one of the great luminaries of the Elizabethan age—a scholar, an orator, a lawyer, a statesman, a philosopher; the first, indeed, of his age and country, and one to whom the nation and mankind in general are much indebted; but I am sorry," I said, "to be obliged to add, that his fame was sullied by one of the meanest of vices."

"Indeed, Mr. C——, you surprise me; why, who could that be?"

"Francis Bacon, Baron Verulam, Viscount St. Albans," I replied.

"Oh, yes! I have heard of him. I have read a great deal about him; he was, indeed, a great man."

"Yes," I continued, for the dreariness of the morning, and the lack of clients, induced the conversation, or, in an old sea-phrase, I had my jawing-tackle on board; "yes, and it is stated by some* that he has been

* It was about this time the hypothesis of Lord Bacon's

robbed of half his fame—that posterity has given to another a renown that has filled the universe—which ought to have belonged to this great man. Yes, sir, from some unknown, and now for ever hidden cause, they seem to argue, that the most capacious mind, the most comprehensive learning, the most fertile imagination, and the most perfect knowledge of the human heart—its springs, motives, and actions, together with the most masterly design, the most eloquent diction, and the most dignified sentiments that the English language ever expressed were produced by the son of a third-rate tradesman in a small provincial town."

"Indeed! Well, I know nothing about that."

"Neither do I, Mr. B——, enough for me that the writings are the product of our language, and will ever be its pride and boast; and though 'Pulmam qui meruit

being the author of some, at least, of Shakspeare's Plays, first made its appearance in the Northern capital.

ferat' is a very good motto, I would rather pass it by and forego a controversy that might tend to disturb the wreath on a brow the entire civilized world has combined to honour."

"I do not exactly understand what you say; but pray tell me who was the second?"

Now, this book-keeper was a respectable tradesman in the town, and had attended this particular coach only, in that capacity, it being originally a subscription-coach and had so remained for many years.

"Why, my dear sir," I said to him, "I fear you will not like the second quite so well." I knew my friend to be a strict religionist, of the Wesleyan persuasion. "The second who claims this as his natal day," I said, "Mr. B——, was a writer who, in our days, has been almost idolized; his works have been very much admired, and he has obtained extraordinary fame as a poet. It has been objected that some of his poems have rather a loose tendency; but his was a master-spirit—he possessed a vigorous understanding and a creative fancy—somewhat tainted with a misanthropic egotism, it must be admitted. His principal weapon was satire, and he handled it with more power than discretion; nevertheless his works will continue to be read by every real lover of poetry, and will for many generations amuse and delight, if not instruct, the masses."

"Who was he, Mr. C——?"

"George Gordon Byron—Lord Byron."

My friend started, and exclaimed:—

"Oh! ah! I do not think so much of him as I do of the other; he has not added much to the moral or religious tenor of our literature."

I was about to argue this point with him, as Mr. Midshipman Easy would say, when he stopped me by asking, who the third was?

"Well, my dear sir, as the clock is about to strike, and it will take me some time to introduce the third to your notice, I must defer it till I see you again."

So, putting on my coat, in which I was assisted by the taciturn porter, I folded up the way-bill, and carefully placed it in my pocket; then walked out, took hold of the reins—the horses being already put to—mounted the box, wished him good morning, and drove off.

The following evening, on my return, he pressed me very hard to tell him who the third celebrated person was to whom I had alluded. I made some excuse—either I had not time then, or I said I hoped he would have discovered it himself; but he never did, nor did I ever tell him, although he repeatedly asked me; and I verily believe he went to his grave uninformed on such a very material point. But, gentle reader, that you may not remain in ignorance of so remarkable a coincidence, one absolutely necessary to give importance to this autobiography, I must confess that *I* was that third person, and must leave it to you to question, pardon, or condemn, the humorous vanity which induced me thus to provoke the curiosity of a simple and inquisitive mind. Yes, on the 22nd of January, in the year 179—, in the ancient and renowned city of Winchester, I first made my appearance on this world's stage, the third of a family that in due time amounted to thirteen.

Should the reader's curiosity be further aroused to wish to know anything of the parentage or genealogy of the humble individual who has thus obtruded himself on his notice, little can be said to gratify it, for little is known to himself. My father, I always understood, was left a penniless orphan when very young. To whose care he was entrusted in his infancy, or how his youth was passed, I never correctly knew; but in mature life, by dint of industry and perseverance, aided by fortuitous circumstances, he had amassed considerable wealth, and had obtained a position in one of the southern counties that his son has long contemplated with unavailing regret, where he, for a time, exercised all the functions, and enjoyed all the social benefits, belonging to the life of a country gentleman—hospitably entertaining a large circle of friends, and, by his constant and liberal employment of the poor, commanding their good word and esteem.

Ingratitude, it is said, is inherent in the heart of man; but when the remains of my father were brought a long distance to be interred in a vault he had built years before for his remains and those of his family, the attendance of the aged villagers, their expressions of respectful remembrance, with their recapitulation of the good he had done when living among them, might, I think, be quoted as an exception.

My mother's patronymic, although herself of humble birth, was the same as that of a family who had been ennobled in the time of the first Charles; and a tradition had obtained currency among us, that she was of the same extraction. This was partly corroborated by a gentleman of this name who, once calling on my father, appeared to me, by his conversation, to be the connecting link between the holder of the title and his far-off and more humble cousins. He bore the commission of Major in one of the Midland Counties militia regiments. I never took any trouble to trace our relationship with this exalted family, but if a noble expression of countenance and personal accomplishments of the highest order were proofs of the alleged descent, my mother possessed them in an eminent degree. "She looked like a duchess?" as a friend of mine said to me, when wishing to explain the impression she made upon him when he first beheld her. But I may be allowed to say, she possessed a far better and juster claim to nobility than either birth, descent, or appearance could give. Exemplary in the performance of all the duties of domestic life, the faith of a true Christian dwelt in her heart, and animated all her actions; and this was daily exemplified either by attention to the requirements of the poor, or by kneeling at the bed-side of the sick and dying. I remember when telling a long absent friend, and one who knew her well, of the place, time, and manner of her death, "Then, sir," said he to me, "departed one of God's best-created beings." She died before a sad fatality buried all my father's property in one whirlpool of destruction; and thus, through the mercy of the Almighty, was spared the misery of witnessing or sharing the fallen estate and almost utter destitution of her family.

I shall now proceed to give a short account of the education, if it deserve the name, that in my boyhood I received, as that generally, if not necessarily, follows the birth and parentage of any one who is desirous of inviting the public attention. It must have been very early in my life when I was placed in a small village school at Sutton Veyney, about three miles from Warminster, in Wiltshire; and I could not have stayed there long, as I have but an indistinct recollection of it, except upon one occasion—a visit of my father to the school, when my master, with his hand upon my head, addressing him, said, "This will make a *sprask* boy, sir!"

I did not then know what this provincialism was intended to convey, any more than I did the cause of my removal; but soon after I found myself at a large school at Twyford, near Winchester, the same village in which Alexander Pope first received the rudiments of those classical acquirements that enabled him to astonish the world with the productions of his immortal pen.

I cannot define the period of my sojourn at this romantic little village, with the silver Itchen washing its flowery meads, upon whose banks we frequently met the Winchester College boys, as they were termed, and were as frequently warned by our ushers of the impropriety of provoking a collision with them; neither can I state what progress I made in those studies that are intended to prepare the mind for something more extensive than the mere knowledge of reading, writing, and arithmetic; but I can recollect nothing to justify the favourable opinion of my capacity which I foolishly fancied my first master had implied. In after-life I met with many of my then school-fellows, who had attained to decent positions; and one or two in particular, who had risen to respectable rank in the army.

I was next removed to a school on the skirts of the market-town of Petersfield, in Hampshire, which I believe availed me but little. I stopped here a twelvemonth; and my master, as I thought, was more fond of surveying the beauties of nature, which here abound, than drilling into obtuse Hampshire boys the mysteries of syntax and prosody. But if I did not advance in knowledge of the classics, I learned, either from him or through the innate love of nature I possessed, how to appreciate the beauties of that salubrious valley, which, surrounded on all sides by what appears to be stupendous hills, seems marked out by nature for the enjoyment of ease and retirement. Often, from the top of Sheet or Ram's Hill, would I stop to observe the fantastic forms the South Downs take on their range towards the east, wondering whether the great Cæsar passed with his legions through any part of this district, on his march in pursuit of the flying Britons; next looked with that delight brilliant objects always inspire on the glittering little lake at their base—saw the white, chalky road winding through the hills in an opposite direction, skirting the little village of Buriton, where is now standing the house in which the historian Gibbon commenced his immortal work; then, crossing the brook, I have walked through the village of Steep, to admire the overhanging woods and deep ravines of Stonor Hill, from whose top, as from a precipice, may be seen one of the finest landscapes this or any other county can afford.

My father, then growing in wealth and prosperity, perceiving, perhaps, that I did not make the progress he had been led to expect, about this time fell in by accident with a reverend divine, who, whatever might have been his doctrine, knew well how to practise good living; and to his care, in a convivial hour, was entrusted my future education.

This Doctor—for he was a D.D.—was eminent as a preacher, though I do not know that he held any benefice, and kept an academy in some repute at Fulham. He, I have heard say, was a well-disposed man, of good average acquirements, and with a fair share of colloquial, as well as pulpit oratory, which he was fond of displaying to those whom he honoured with his company, and who might benefit by his homilies—but they were not his scholars; he left them generally to the care of his ushers; and never shall I forget the torments I suffered from the punishment the senior pedagogue from some particular dislike, or from the love of inflicting pain, thought proper frequently to visit me with—unknown, I was sure, to his principal.

However, in the course of the first twelvemonths of my stay, the principal died, and the scholars were sent home, some of them never to return. This was not my case; at the request of the widow I was allowed to remain, and after a little time the school was conducted by a gentleman who had graduated at Oxford. Then, indeed, did a revolution take place in that afterwards most excellent school—and then did my young mind first begin to find pleasure in learning. The petty tyrant who had exercised such arbitrary and cruel rule, always carrying in his pocket a peculiar instrument of punishment of his own invention, with which he struck terror and hatred into the hearts of most of the scholars—to my great relief and joy was sent away. No usher was allowed to strike a boy under any circumstances. Chastisement was administered by the master's hand alone, and so superior was the system this excellent man judiciously adopted, that the cries of a delinquent were seldom heard. By his easy and temperate method, learning was made attractive to even the unwilling mind. The most sullen temper was subdued by his kind and persuasive manner. He was at once a well-bred gentleman, an accomplished scholar, and a sincere Christian, and possessed by nature the power of drawing and attaching to him the affection as well as the obedience and esteem of his pupils. Naturally of an inquisitive disposition, I was led by this good man to drink at the fountain of knowledge. It is true I could sip but little, and but little I may have retained, through a long and fitful existence; but young though I was, I can well remember he was the first to pour into my heart, from the stream of ancient lore, the sweet, refreshing drops of an intellectual nectar. To him I am indebted for imbibing a just appreciation of the value of the learning, which harsh and untoward circumstances gave subsequently to the winds. I need only add, that during the four years I was at his academy I may truly point to the last two as being the most happy of my life. But this was not to last. At the commencement of the summer vacation, in the year 1806, I took my leave of this worthy person, little thinking that I should never again touch the hand of one who had directed and encouraged my studious disposition, had so kindly applauded my assiduity, and expressed his gratification at the progress I had made—little supposing I should never look upon those mild, intelligent features again—but so it was. I remember to have heard from a near relative of his, for whom I formed a sincere friendship some few years afterwards, of his early death. The intelligence caused me to recall to mind his many virtues and commanding talents, and ever since to cherish for them the greatest respect.

My trunk having been sent by the carrier overnight to the office in London, I walked, in company with one of the ushers, over Putney Bridge, and awaited on Wimbledon Common the coming by of the coach that was to convey me to my father's dwelling, not dreaming of the sudden turn my fortune or destiny was about to take.

I have been on many roads in almost every part of England, and in none have I ever witnessed finer scenery than the ride from London to Portsmouth afforded. To be seen to perfection, it must be on a fine day from the top of a stage-coach. Haldown on the road from Exeter to Plymouth may rival it in extent, and Moranscourt Hill on that to Hastings in richness and splendour, but neither of those lengthened rides can come up to it in that diversified and real picturesque beauty, to which my pen must fail to do justice. The vehicle I mounted was not of the most elegant build, and was certainly capable of those great improvements that were so freely bestowed on such carriages before they were quite sent off the road; neither was the pace anything like what was afterwards reached—thirteen or fourteen hours accomplishing the seventy-two miles, subsequently done in seven or eight; still it was considered a great accommodation and a good equipment in those days. The coachman, by whose side I sat, had particular charge concerning me, and was pleased to point out the objects most worthy of notice.

Crossing the Common, where was exposed to view on a gibbet the remains of a celebrated highwayman, called Jerry Abbershaw, at whose dangling chains and half-decayed bones in our holiday walks I had cast many a stone, we ascended Kingston-hill, leaving Coombe Wood, the seat of Lord Hawkesbury, afterwards the Earl of Liverpool, on the left, and Richmond Park on the right, from whence you have a wide extent of prospect—the Thames winding its majestic course to the great metropolis from the foot of an eminence, where stands the lofty towers of Windsor Castle, (the residence of our sovereigns for centuries), first washing with its yet unpolluted waters the villas of Pope and Horace Walpole.

Passing through the old and ill-paved town of Kingston, where rests the rude stone on which the Saxon monarch sat at his coronation,* on the opposite side of the river

* This remarkable relic has of late been surrounded by an iron palisade, the better to preserve to remote posterity so singular a memorial of the rude simplicity of our Saxon ancestors. It may be said to represent the lasting solidity of a constitutional monarchy, of which it is aptly the foundation-stone.

stands the stately edifice of Hampton Court Palace, with its *parterres*, its labyrinths, and its well-trained vines. Crossing a flat, called Ditton Marsh, at Esher, on the left the fine Grecian structure of Claremont meets the eye, then the property of Mr. Ellis, afterwards Lord Seaford; since the scene of the premature death of the lamented Princess Charlotte of Wales, and now the residence of Amelie, late Queen of the French.

Proceeding through the post-town of Cobham, you see Paine's Hill, once the seat of Colonel Luttrel, often mentioned by the celebrated Junius, but then the property of a member of the same family—the Earl of Carhampton. Onward, through Ripley, you pass the parks of Lords King (now Earl Lovelace), and Onslow, the one on the left, the other on the right, till you come to the county town of Guildford, from whence, right and left, you have delightful views of the neighbouring Surrey hills.

Crossing the Wye, and passing through Godalming, with the woody heights of Busbridge on the left—then the seat of Mr. Hare Townsend, the friend and companion of the great Charles Fox—the road opens on a wide, extensive heath, with a continuous rise. Leaving Pepper Harrow, the seat of Lord Middleton, on the right, it winds round a deep dell, known as the Devil's Punch-Bowl, till it reaches the summit, called the Hind's Head: on the top of which stood another of those "hanging woods" frequent in the latter part of the eighteenth century, and not totally lost sight of till long after the commencement of the nineteenth—this was a tripartite erection—and the names of the parties and their crime are recorded on a stone still standing by the side of the bowl, down which they dragged their victim. Looking down the deep declivity that forms the side of this spacious circular ravine, here and there you might see peasant boys gathering berries, and a very little stretch of imagination, will enable you to recall a familiar paragraph from "Lear," and almost realize the picture the poet has so graphically drawn:—

> "Half-way down
> Hangs one that gathers samphire: dreadful trade!
> Methinks he seems no bigger than his head."

Elevated about 1,000 feet above the level of the sea, you have one of the most magnificent and picturesque views the mind can contemplate from such a position. In vain the eye attempts to rest upon any particular object, except at its extreme points. On the right the hill that bounds the sight in that direction, upholds the little town of Nettlebed in Oxfordshire; while on the left the eye can distinctly perceive an object in Tonbridge Wells, at a distance of 130 miles, across steep hills and deep ravines; heath and forest, glebe and meadow, presenting a landscape that bids defiance to the art of man to describe.

I cannot refrain from recording the impression made on my mind by the beauty of this delightful scenery. I have since often enjoyed it, and many others must have admired it, but it is now for ever closed to the traveller by rail.

Proceeding at a more rapid pace down the descent over what would appear, from the rich yellow flowering of the furze, then in the fulness of its bloom, to be the historical field of the cloth of gold, we reached the little hamlet of Liphook, and stopped at the "Anchor"—a well-known posting-house—half-an-hour to dine. Starting from thence, we trotted briskly on an undulating road, leaving the seat called Hollycombe, the property of Mr., now Sir C. Taylor, on the left, with sight of Woolmer Forest, the scene of White's natural history of Selborne, on the right, and a most lovely romantic valley, bounded by lofty hills in the distance, to the town of Petersfield, a locality I have already mentioned; and then, after an additional two hours' ride through and over the downs, occasionally catching a glimpse of the element that has added so much to the glory and safety of our country; we enjoyed a most splendid view from Portsdown Hill, comprising Portsmouth harbour, Spithead, and the Isle of Wight—and at last arrived safely at Portsmouth.

My father having a very good house in the High Street, was residing there during some addition or repairs he was making at his place in the country. Something appeared to have disturbed him, for I had scarcely had time to enjoy the welcome with which I was received by other members of my family, when somewhat harshly he intimated the necessity of my preparing at once to do something in the way of earning my own subsistence; and stated that he had already made arrangements for my quitting home with this object. At this unexpected announcement I burst into tears, and implored him to revoke his decision. A captain in the Royal Navy called in, and after the customary salutation, seeing my distress, said, in a bluff manner:—

"What's the matter with the lad?" Having been informed of the cause of my grief—for grief it really was—addressing me, he asked, "Will you go to sea with me, my boy?"

Dashing the tears from my eyes, I replied, in an audible voice, "Yes, sir."

Without further consideration or consultation the affair was arranged. This was on Wednesday evening. On Sunday morning following I was outside the Isle of Wight, steering down Channel with a flowing sheet.

And thus, gentle reader, ended my education, in the common acceptation of that term.

CHAPTER II.

THE VOYAGE OUT.

The Departure and Outfit—A Fourth-rate Man-of-War—Captain, Officers, and Crew—Sea-sickness—The Quarter-deck—The Cock-pit—An Accident—Lubber's Hole—The Schoolmaster—Midshipmen—Rio de Janeiro—An Extraordinary Feat—A False Alarm—The Captain's Table—A Court-martial, Sentence, and Execution—Scenes in the Gun-room and in the Captain's Cabin—A Pleasant Time—The Middle Watch—Fore and Afternoon Watches—The First Lieutenant—Corporal Punishment—The Haven.

The bustle of preparation consequent upon a sudden and hasty departure on a voyage of uncertain duration, causes such a degree of excitement among all the members of a family, both young and old, as to divert their thoughts from dwelling on the dreaded "farewell," and serves to shield the heart from the effects of the sorrowful anticipation of a long separation.

The determination thus taken, was without reference to the fitness of my capacity, either of mind or body, for such a profession, or to the future fate of a boy twelve years and a half old. The ship being under sailing orders, I was soon attired in the uniform of a midshipman of the Royal Navy, with a cocked-hat on my head, and a dirk by my side, and was not a little proud of my appearance. In the meantime, my kind parents were busily employed in purchasing my outfit, in providing me everything I did want, and many things I did not want, that afterwards conduced to the especial sport and jests of my messmates.

The ship I went on board, after taking leave of my friends, was one of the worst class of two-deckers—high out of the water, short, wall-sided, with a bluff bow, and a square stern. She was the last ship built of that class, and had been recently launched from Portsmouth dockyard. The improvement in our naval architecture may date from this time, when the superior models of the French and Spanish ships, taken during the late war, invited the attention of the Admiralty or Navy Board to their particular structure, and soon condemned such vessels as I have named to serve as hospital or convict-ships.

On board of a man-of-war, then, of the fourth class, I was admitted as a supernumerary midshipman, under the especial charge of the captain, who bore the family name of, and was closely connected with, an Irish earldom.* The ward-room officers consisted of four lieutenants, a master, a doctor, a purser, and two marine officers. The cockpit contained, with midshipmen, master's mates, doctor's mates, and captain's clerk, in all about twenty, while the

* Thomas Gordon Caulfield.

crew consisted of about five hundred, including warrant, petty officers and idlers, most of them first-class seamen, having been pressed from a homeward-bound East India fleet in the Downs; and no finer crew ever went to sea in a British man-of-war.

Our captain's orders were to take charge of a fleet of Indiamen, South-Seamen, &c., that had assembled at the Motherbank, and convoy them to their destination, which was principally Calcutta.

Being thought too young to join either the starboard or larboard mess in the cockpit, I, with two other youngsters as we were termed, were committed to the care of the gunner—a hard-featured, weather-beaten Scotchman, though rough, yet kind in his manner.

No sooner was the anchor weighed and the ship under easy sail, than I was seized with a nausea that soon extinguished all feelings of regret at leaving my home—indeed, almost all remembrance of that home and its inmates. I suffered from that dreadful sea-sickness three days, refusing all sustenance, till, on my partial recovery, the gunner gave me a cup of strong tea without either sugar or milk. I drank it, but I cannot recall what effect it had towards my restoration; nevertheless so did I loathe his remedy, that I have never since touched, nor could I ever be persuaded again to taste, that highly-prized beverage, though more than half a century has elapsed —such is the force of early impression, combined perhaps with prejudice.

Had I any particular emotions either of diffidence, or gratification, or pride, on my first coming on deck and viewing the wide expanse of waters, covered as it was by innumerable vessels spreading their white canvas to the wind, they were soon dissipated by the strict order that was kept on one side of the quarter-deck, and by the jocose observations, some of kindness, some of scorn, made by persons on the other. To avoid their not very pleasing jests I ascended the poop ladder; and the captain seeing me, gave the first-lieutenant instructions that my earliest duty should be to attend and assist the signal officer, who was then present arranging the different party-coloured pieces of bunting, and immediately commenced his tuition; and I had the good fortune soon to ingratiate myself with one whom I afterwards found to be a thorough-bred gentleman, and a most excellent officer.*

The cockpit of a man-of-war may be justly termed the school of our naval heroes, where the peculiarities of mind and temper are sure to be developed. The characters and dispositions of its different inmates, their amusements and their feuds, have been so graphically described by Captain Marryat and other nautical novelists, that I can only testify to the general truth of their delineations. It was

* Lieutenant Samuel Greenway.

some little time before I was admitted among them, and more before I became thoroughly acquainted with the usages of so unique an assemblage as a midshipman's mess, or acquired anything like a perfect knowledge of those who composed it.

An old seventy-four, called the "Russell," with an additional fleet of merchantmen, had joined us off Plymouth; so that together we made a considerable flotilla, not only in numbers, but in wealth. Our sail to the island of Madeira, where we stayed but two days, was marked with only one incident worthy of recording; my time was taken up principally in assisting to make and repeat signals, to keep the convoy together, to prevent them straggling too much to windward or to leeward, and to compel the sternmost to make more sail. In the evening the crew were exercised at the guns, or sometimes in reefing topsails; and it was upon one of the last occasions, when the captain had ordered the men up aloft a second time in consequence of their not being smart enough to please him, that one of our best men fell from the main topsail yard-arm on to the larboard gangway, and was killed on the spot. I was standing by the side of the captain on the poop at the time, and when he went down the ladder on to the quarter-deck into his cabin, his face covered with his hands, I did not envy him his feelings.

I cannot boast of any progress I made in my profession during this short run, unless it be that I was able to reach the main or mizen top, though not by the way used by the topmen, the futtock shrowds, but through "Lubbers' hole," as the sailors call the open space in that lofty platform.

While at Madeira our captain induced his brother of the "Russell" to let us have the assistance of a schoolmaster he had on board, for a few weeks; and during the run to Rio Janeiro he assembled the midshipmen every day in his cabin to be instructed in navigation. My aptitude for learning had not forsaken me, and I quickly left my competitors for scientific acquirements a long way behind. Geometry, Trigonometry, and Mensuration were soon mastered, so well had I been prepared at the school I had so recently and so reluctantly quitted. At the end of six weeks I was as capable of taking and working a lunar observation as any officer in the ship—much to the annoyance of many of my brother midshipmen, my seniors in age and service; and having obtained a greater share of notice in consequence, did not add to my own social comfort or happiness. Nevertheless, confident, or vain, perhaps, of the superiority I had gained, I treated their jeers and their contumely with all the contempt I could assume, though I was frequently provoked to words of recrimination and abuse.

One of these, whose sponsors had thought proper to bestow on him the lofty baptismal name of Theophilus Caractacus, was a tall, gawky youth, of about eighteen, who, whatever his pretensions were to emulate the deeds of his illustrious namesake in arms, certainly bid fair to be on a level with him in his intellectual capacity—for the knowledge of letters seemed as foreign to him, as they were to the ancient Briton, from whom, like other Welchmen, he boasted his descent. If, by the other appellation, it was intended that he should in his manhood bear any resemblance to a name known in the early history of our creed, his friends must have been disappointed, for meekness and charity were not to be reckoned among his virtues. This man or youth was my particular bane, and fortunate was it for me, perhaps, that I did not belong to the same mess, for, although the disproportion of our physical powers precluded, for shame's sake and the fear of others more his equals, the probability of any personal encounter, still, when assembled on the poop or quarter-deck to take an altitude at noon, his venom would display itself in some arrogant expressions on the inequality of our births; and my angry, and sometimes pithy, allusions to his gross ignorance would excite general sympathy, while some happy travestie on his high-sounding name would create the laughter of our superior officers.

Another, with whom I was more immediately associated, for he was one of the three committed to the care of the gunner, was a true scion of the aristocracy, had some pretensions to the birth of a gentleman, and would be possessed, on coming of age, of considerable property. This hero in embryo would take frequent opportunities of showing his personal dislike, as well as his contempt, for all beneath him in birth and connections. He was my superior in age by two or three years, and I should have fared badly with this haughty, supercilious boy, as he then was, had it not been for the fellow-feeling, that afterwards ripened into a brotherly friendship, existing between myself and the third individual, who with us constituted our little mess; and the severe remonstrance sometimes administered by our kind-hearted president, who himself had no particular regard or respect for youths of aristocratic bearing.

This promising young officer, on the arrival of the ship at Madras, told the captain the service was not fit for a gentleman, and begged to be invalided home; this was immediately granted. He quitted the ship unregretted by either officers or crew, and I have never seen him from that time. I believe he afterwards entered the army, which he left on some similar pretence; his name was well known in the fashionable circles for some few years, and was mentioned in connection with the celebrated ball at Brussels, prior to the battle of Waterloo, where the charms of Lady Frances Wedderburn Webster attracted the attention of the hero of that eventful day.

The third of my associates was a fine, handsome lad, a little above my own age, fresh from the sister isle, of primitive ideas, but of a noble and generous nature. He was also a *protégé* of the captain's, and was extremely well connected. I remember it was a standing joke against him, which he always took with habitual good humour, that one day at the captain's table he attempted to invert the process of eating asparagus, by squeezing the palatable part between his fingers, and putting the less succulent end to his lips; the loud laughter of the captain's guests soon corrected the mistake.

Nevertheless, his simple and unsophisticated manner gained him friends; and, had his life been spared, he would have been a star in the firmament of the profession, which he followed with much ardour and devotion. He was sent away in a boat with two others, under the command of a lieutenant and boatswain, to cut out and destroy some Malay praams, that had taken shelter under the high land on the coast of Sumatra. The lieutenant was the first to climb the bows of the pirate; my poor friend followed him, when the foremost Malay made a thrust with his spear, which passing through the lieutenant's trousers, entered the chest of this brave youth, and caused him to fall backwards; the boatswain, whose name I remember was Thomas George, a fine athletic fellow, mounting the deck at the moment, with his cutlass severed the fellow's head from his body. The rascals soon ran below; and on battening down the hatches to secure them and mustering the crew, only one was missing, and that was my most esteemed friend.

It was supposed that from the force of the spear alone he must have fallen between the praam and the gunwale of his own boat, and, from his body not being found, have met a watery grave. His loss was sincerely lamented by captain, officers, and crew. I was not a spectator of this sharp and successful encounter; but it was as the lieutenant in command related it to me. At parting, I had exchanged seals with this amiable youth, and in doing so we both fondly anticipated some future happy meeting, but that was not to be in this world.*

But this is anticipating my story. On casting anchor in the harbour of Rio de Janeiro—then the principal trading port in the Brazils, and subject to the Crown of Portugal, now the capital of an extensive and rising empire—we found three line-of-battle-ships and a frigate, with the flag of Admiral Hartsinck, belonging to the Batavian Republic, who had, at the bidding of

* He was Luke Burgh.—Some few years afterwards, I read with much gratification the advancement of a military officer of the same name, Sir Ulysses Burgh, whom I took to be his elder brother, to the peerage of the United Kingdom, by the title of Lord Downes. He had served on the staff of the great Duke, throughout his campaigns in the Peninsula.

the French Government, recently declared war against us. About three days after our arrival we were joined by two new seventy-fours, the "Albion," and the "Sceptre," from England, sent out to reinforce the squadron in the East Indies, under Admiral Rainier. This was considered a very timely arrival for us, as, unless we had been reinforced, we must have remained there—for, although three days must elapse between the sailing of two hostile fleets from a neutral port, we could not have left without the certainty of being overtaken by the enemy, as several of our convoy were very dull sailers. As it was, we now considered ourselves quite a match for them, and, should they dare to pursue us, had made up our minds to give them a warm reception. Nevertheless, while we were laying there together, every civility passed between the senior officers of the two hostile fleets. Independent of balls, and fêtes, and dinners on shore, given by the Portuguese authorities, in which no preference was shewn to either nation, a reciprocity of visits daily took place on board one or other of the men-of-war, each taking it by turn to entertain the officers of the other; while the midshipmen would endeavour to surpass each other in feats of daring agility on the masts, yards, and rigging of their respective ships. Hence the foundation, if not the truth, of that feat of our countryman that has since obtained general circulation, but is set down by people on shore as nothing better than a Joe Miller or a Munchausen.

The Dutch, whatever may be the distinguishing features of their more mature age, are in their youth and on the water particularly bold and active. Upon the occasion I am now relating, one of the Dutch midshipmen ascended to the main-royal mast-head and sat at his ease on the truck, which in shape and size resembles a small round table, and between it and the sky there is nothing. One of ours, on seeing this, immediately ran up the rigging, and with great apparent ease and confidence, stood upon the truck, and waved his hat in defiance. This was not to be borne, for the Dutch boy, with wonderful daring and activity, turned himself over, and stood upon his head, with his heels towards the heavens, to the amazement of the crews of the other ships, both English and Dutch. Determined not to be outdone, with more spirit than discretion, the British youth attempted the same exhibition, but not being so clever at gymnastics as his rival, he toppled over and fell, to the great momentary alarm of his shipmates; but first a stay, then a backstay or bowline, breaking his fall, he came safe on deck; when, jumping up and snapping his fingers at the Dutch line-of-battleship, with great presence of mind, he said, "There, gentlemen, do that if you can!" The ship was not within hearing, nor could the crew have understood our language, but the loud shouts of laughter and exultation this feat elicited from both officers and men, announced to their astonished minds that an Englishman was not to be beaten at that or any other game.

After three weeks' stay at this hospitable port, during which time we were employed in refitting our rigging and replenishing the water-casks, we set sail some time in September—the other three men-of-war and convoy in company—for our ultimate destination.

We had not much expectation of Admiral Hartsinck's following us, though we always kept a sharp look-out night and day, but we saw nothing of him or his squadron. We were stationed in the rear of the convoy, to give timely notice of the approach of an enemy, as well as to whip up and cover the stragglers; when one night, observing what we took to be a large ship on our larboard quarter, and not being able to make her out, we piped all hands to quarters, and cleared ship for action. The captain and officers on the deck were intent on observing her with their night-glasses. The lower deck guns were run out, and we every minute expected a broadside, and were prepared to return it. To our great surprise and disappointment, upon a closer inspection she turned out to be one of our own convoy, that had got out of the order of sailing, and had straggled away from the rest of the fleet; and not understanding our night signals or not answering them, she had caused us to mistake her for an enemy.

About a week after we had left Rio, thinking there was no chance of the Dutch squadron molesting us, the "Albion" and "Sceptre" made signal to part company, and, crowding all sail, were hull down at sunset, and next morning were nowhere to be seen.

I must here relate a circumstance of not very frequent occurrence in those days in a man-of-war, when long voyages were unavoidable, and the captain's power unlimited, but is now I believe out of the scale of probability: it was one, too, that materially altered my position. Two of our midshipmen were not on very good terms with the captain. One had refused his invitation to breakfast, which being reported to the captain, and, as I understood, his refusal or excuse being highly coloured by the valet or steward (who to the best of my recollection was either Swiss or French) his commander said that he never knew a midshipman in his life but what would eat *two* breakfasts; consequently he fell into disfavour: the other had been so for some time. It was the custom of the service then, and I believe it is so still, for one of the midshipmen to breakfast and another to dine with the captain every day; they were selected in turn, the first from the morning, the other from the forenoon watch.

In consequence of the expected long run to Calcutta, that the dull sailing of the convoy had caused to be of unusual duration, and there being no port at which we could possibly touch before reaching the Bay of Bengal—the Cape of Good Hope being at that time in the hands of the Dutch, it having been restored to them at the peace of Amiens—it was thought necessary to put the ship's company, officers included, (for there is no distinction in these cases,) on a short allowance of water.

Now it came to the turn of a young Irishman, who had served about half his time, by the name of Nixon, to dine with the captain, a day or two after; and in the course of conversation at the table he was asked how the young gentlemen, meaning the midshipmens' mess, did with the minimum of water to which they were restricted. In the simple and ingenuous manner that was natural to him, he replied, "Oh, capital! very well—indeed, they could do with half the quantity." Whether the captain took him at his word and acted accordingly,

I cannot at this distance of time pretend to say, but on his retiring from the table and coming below, his messmates flocked round him, requesting to know, as was usual with them, what the captain talked about; when he repeated the conversation, and foolishly divulged the error he had committed.

Upon this the majority of the mess took umbrage, and accused him of being the cause, from his folly or obsequiousness, in attempting thus to gain favour with the captain, of the privations they were about to suffer for the remainder of the voyage; and upon one or two of them saying he ought to have a good licking, it was quickly resolved, at the instigation of the doctor's mate, that he should be tried by a court-martial of six of the elders of the mess, the senior master's mate to be the president.

This mock trial was soon over; he being convicted by his own confession, there was no necessity for any further evidence; and the president, after a short consultation, sentenced him, in nautical language, to be cobbed—a punishment, I believe, only known on board ship. Resistance was useless, and he was immediately seized up to the aftermost gun on the lower deck; the captain having given the gun-room to the midshipmen for their better accommodation, it being more freely ventilated than the cockpit, consequently more healthy, particularly in a tropical climate.

By the artful advice of the doctor's mate, who was no friend to the youth, and owed him a grudge, everyone in the two messes was included in the infliction of this punishment, on the pain of being served the same, or sent to Coventry.

The instrument selected for the purpose was what is called by the ship's cook the "Burgoo-stirrer;" in shape it resembles a large battledore, and is generally made of some hard wood. With this formidable weapon each one was to give the culprit six blows upon the most fleshy part of his body—which, though not uncovered, presented, from the attitude to which he was confined, an unmistakable mark.

The master's mate—a fine young man, about nineteen or twenty years of age, and nearly six feet high,* and who had acted as president, was the first to put the sentence in force; and the victim writhed and twisted under his powerful blows, though his proud heart would not suffer his lips to utter a word of complaint. Two or three others followed, when, either from compassion or want of muscular power, they did not draw forth from the sufferer any particular signs of anguish; but when the doctor's mate, a tall, raw-boned, long-armed Scotchman, took the implement of torture, and administered his blows, with all the strength a sinewy arm and a malignant spirit could give, the poor youth, no longer able to con-

* This young man in time rose to the rank of Post-Captain, Sir John Marshall, and was a Knight-Commander of the Bath at his decease.

tain himself, absolutely roared with pain. The punishment over, the prisoner was cast off, when he immediately ascended to the captain's cabin.

I was a silent spectator of this specimen of Lynch law, as it may be termed, and was not thought of importance enough to be included in the unanimity with which the whole proceeding was conducted; but I looked with something between compassion for the delinquent and anger and horror at the two principal perpetrators in this, to me, diabolical affair, and marked the fearful silence that reigned among them, till they were one and all summoned to the captain's presence.

I followed, as did my two young messmates, who had been for the same reason excluded with myself from any participation in the crime or folly of the others. Those, also, who fortunately had the watch on deck at the time of this unjust assumption of authority and act of downright cruelty, were also called in.

The first lieutenant stood by the side of the captain, as did the doctor and purser; the master, and most of the other officers, were also in the cabin, when their commander expressed himself in an angry tone, and in the strongest terms of reprobation at their recent conduct; condemning it as unworthy the character of gentlemen's sons, at variance with the rules of the service, and totally subversive of that good feeling that should actuate young men who were desirous of advancing in the profession; and on that account, if on no other, should cultivate each other's friendship and good-will.

For this grave offence, which he told them he could not stigmatize too strongly, he said that he should from that hour disrate all who had been guilty of such a disgraceful conspiracy; and that upon his arrival in India on the station he should apply to the

Admiral for a court-martial of a little different nature from that they had concocted, when they would most assuredly be dismissed the service. In the meantime, they were not to do duty any more as officers on board his ship, nor were they to appear on the quarter-deck. This sentence, however severe it may be thought, was put in force immediately by the captain calling in his clerk, who in their presence erased their names from the list of petty officers in the ship's books, reducing them to the rank of A. B. or O. S., in which capacity some of them were compelled to do duty; one of them, I remember, who had in the early part of the voyage fallen under the captain's displeasure, was put in the foretop.

This was the unfortunate youth who could not eat two breakfasts. "Henry Parry," bawled out the first lieutenant, "you will do duty in the foretop starboard watch; and if you don't answer to your muster, I'll start you as I would any other foremast man."

"Hard cheese for a gentleman's son," said one or two of his messmates; but he submitted, and did his duty so well, that one evening, when reefing topsails, the captain observing him said, addressing the first-lieutenant, Graves,

"Who is that smart lad on the fore-topsail yard-arm, at the starboard ear-ring?"

"That's Parry, sir."

"Call him down," said the captain, then first relenting, "and send him aft."

This gentleman is now on the reserved list of commanders, and the author has had an opportunity of renewing his acquaintance, after an interval of more than forty years.

This done, they left the cabin, when the captain, turning to the sufferer, who stood with tears in his eyes, rubbing the part which had been the seat of so much pain, admonished him, in very strong terms, on the impropriety of his conduct, in repeating or divulging anything he might have heard at his table. He then addressed us youngsters, and warned us never to be guilty of the same thing; so saying, he waved his hand, when we bowed and left the cabin.

And never have I forgotten the lesson thus early implanted in my mind, which is applicable to all stations and ages; for mischief, even to death, has been caused by words being incautiously repeated. The whole scene, from the beginning to end, made such an impression on me, that it is as fresh in my memory as if it had happened but yesterday.

A fatal instance of imprudence occurred on the West India station, a few years after I left the service; and although I believe it has been recorded by one or more of our nautical novelists, it may not be considered out of course repeated here, as it was related to me by an old shipmate of mine, who was, I believe, an eye-witness, not many months after it happened — I allude to a duel that took place between Captain Stackpole of the "Statira" frigate, and a lieutenant of another of H. M. ships on the same station, named "Cecil." The captain was considered a dead shot, having sailed as a lieutenant with that celebrated duellist, Captain Macnamara, who, it may be remembered by some of the oldest of my readers, killed Colonel Montgomery; and though himself wounded, was tried with his second at the Old Bailey for that affair.

It was their custom, when at sea, to practise pistol-shooting, by putting a solitary fowl in a hen-coop, placed prominently before the others on the spars—

that is between the main and foremasts; a little barley would be strewed in the trough, and when the bird put its head out to feed, it presented a fair mark to the two officers who stood on the poop, when one or the other seldom missed; and this was repeated till a sufficient number had been killed, to supply the captain's and ward-room officers' tables. By this method they became experienced and excellent marksmen.

The captain had heard from some officious talebearer, that a young and excellent officer had said, when speaking of him, (Captain S.,) that he was a good fellow enough, but that he could pull the long bow; which the generality of my readers will at once understand, means that he could exaggerate, and perhaps a little more. This, it seems, the captain cherished in his memory. One day being at anchor in Port-Royal, Jamaica, a man-of-war was seen steering for the harbour, and upon her number being made known, he recognized the ship of which his intended victim was first-lieutenant. He immediately sent a note on board, stating the nature of the offence, and demanding a written apology, or a meeting. The lieutenant, who bore an excellent character, as an officer and a gentleman, returned for answer, that he had no recollection of having used the words imputed to him ; but if he had incautiously done so, he was ready to make a verbal apology.

This did not satisfy the captain, who would have nothing short of a written apology ; this again the lieutenant absolutely refused, saying, to any other man but Captain S. he would readily subscribe to the terms proposed, but to him never, as, from his well-known practice, his doing so would be attributed to cowardice, and for ever ruin him in the service.

Accordingly a meeting was appointed. In going to the ground, Capt. S. met his adversary's captain; he stopped, and in the most confident manner said, "I am compelled to deprive you of the services of your first-lieutenant for a short time — I shall only wing him;" and then walked on to the spot, where he found the lieutenant waiting with his friend. The ground was measured, the pistols delivered by the seconds, and each took his position. So unacquainted was the lieutenant with the nature of this detestable practice of settling disputes, that he presented his front to his adversary, which the captain observing, said in a loud voice, "Shew me your feather edge, sir, or I'll shoot you as dead as a rat." Upon this, by direction of his second, he adjusted his position, and on the signal being given they both fired. The lieutenant stood unhurt; while the captain fell, exclaiming something expressive of his surprise at having missed him, and died before he was carried off the ground.

The words which the great Napoleon said, when General Moreau was mortally wounded by a cannon-ball before the walls of Dresden, "Surely the finger of Providence was there," may much more justly be applied on this occasion. The body of Capt. S. was interred in the burying-ground at Port-Royal, and in one short year after, his adversary lay by his side, having died of yellow fever.

The day after our assembly in the captain's cabin the order of the watch was re-arranged, and we three, who were now raised from supernumeraries to the rank of full midshipmen, were, with the junior master's mate, (who, wise in his generation, had either cunningly or accidentally avoided committing himself as the others had done,) were put into the third-lieutenant's watch, the officer who from the beginning had taken me under his kind protection. Then did my time pass pleasantly enough; feeling a little my importance, as forecastle midshipman, I thought I was gaining ground on the great Caractacus, who had but so recently occupied that post, and who was now debarred, with the others who had been disrated from speaking to us, either off or on duty. Added to the satisfaction of being out of reach of such annoyance, the haughty demeanour of the other individual I have before alluded to, was somewhat softened down towards me, if not totally changed, by the tact and impartial conduct of the officer of our watch, who would see no difference, and make no distinction between us, and did all he could to make our duties light and our time happy.

Often in the middle watch, when crossing the South Atlantic, with the trade wind blowing steadily and constantly from one point of the compass, little or no alteration in the trim of the sails or quantity of canvas was necessary, under a sky sparkling with a brilliancy unknown in the northern hemisphere, and nothing was heard but the reply of the man at the helm to the quartermaster. This officer would assemble us on the poop, and, sending to his cabin for a liquor-case, he would invite us all to fill our glasses, and then cause each of us to sing a song, himself joining in the chorus; sometimes varying the amusement by exercising his wit good-humouredly on my Hibernian friend; at others with anecdotes gained from his own experience in the service, or by some happy allusion to those we had left behind.

The greater part of the morning watch in those warm latitudes and comparatively smooth seas I spent in climbing the masts and rigging; and I had now gained sufficient courage and confidence to reach the truck, but not to rival the feats of either the Dutch or the English midshipman.

In the fore and afternoon—that is, when it was my watch upon deck—I would employ myself in learning to knot and splice, under the tuition of the captain of the forecastle—a fine specimen of a British sailor; and frequently learn from the boatswain, who took pleasure in instructing me, the names and use of the different ropes, the marks on the lead line, and every part of practical seamanship. Indeed, with the crew generally I was an especial favourite, who, with but one or two exceptions, were quiet and orderly men, of sober and obedient habits, and, with every characteristic of British sailors, united a respect for, and attachment to, their officers.

The first-lieutenant, who, under the captain, is the principal agent for creating and maintaining a proper discipline in the ship, was a man somewhere about thirty years of age, not tall, but very stout, of a fine open countenance, and with lungs that did not require a speaking-trumpet to make his voice heard either aloft or on board any strange ship we had occasion to hail. He was every inch a sailor; and, from the straightforward, officer-like, and impartial manner in which he carried on the duties in all the various departments of the ship, had obtained among the men the soubriquet of "Honest Joe," though that was not his baptismal name; and to his thorough knowledge of the service, as well as to his proper way of treating men who were their country's boast, may be attributed the infrequency of corporeal punishment among them. I remember but one instance of it occurring during our voyage out from Rio Janeiro, and that was under peculiar circumstances.

One of the boatswain's mates, who had recently been promoted to that office, was a man of arrogant deportment, and too fond of exercising his authority over men his equals in everything but rank. Upon one occasion he called one of the men on the forecastle a lazy lubber, and other opprobrious epithets, and threatened to start him; whereupon the man, not being able to keep his temper, struck him with his fist, and knocked him down.

Now, to strike your superior officer is death by the articles of war, which the captain took care to have read every Sunday on the quarterdeck. Upon this affair being reported, the man was immediately put in irons; and the next day at noon all hands were piped for punishment, and the offender was brought to the gangway by the master-at-arms. He was ordered to strip, which he did without a word, and was seized up; when the captain, who was not by any means a Tartar, animadverted strongly on the offence that he had committed, by which he had subjected himself to the greatest penalty known to martial law; but in consequence of the character he bore, he had commuted his punishment, and therefore ordered him to receive two dozen lashes, for, he added, he should not be doing his duty were he to pass over such a breach of discipline.

He, who was as good a seaman as any in the ship, received the amount of his sentence without flinching, and without a word being spoken by any of the officers, who one and all deeply sympathised with the sufferer, while a tear was seen to trickle down the cheek of honest old Joe.

Upon the man's being cast off, the captain addressed the boatswain's mate, and told him that he had been the means of one of the best men in the ship being flogged; that, as he found him not fit to be trusted with authority, he should incapacitate him from committing the same thing again, by disrating him from the office he then held; and he was disrated accordingly, much to the satisfaction of both officers and men.

This, I believe, was the only instance of corporeal punishment we had in our long run out—a system of punishment that never should be resorted to hardly under any circumstances, as a too frequent application of it tends to debase the minds of the men, and render them callous to every sentiment of pride in their calling, or regard for their country, while it renders the officers familiar with acts that are degrading to humanity. Much to the credit of our naval discipline, it is now but little practised.

After a voyage of more than eight months at sea, except the three weeks we were at Rio Janeiro, we cast anchor in the Hooghley, in the month of February, 1804, first having made Dondra Head, where the "Russell" parted company with the Madras division of the convoy.

CHAPTER III.

THE VOYAGE HOME.

Day-Dreams—The Shark and the Dolphin—Yarns—A Hard Hit—The Armourer's Chest—Calcutta– The Marquis Wellesley — The Return — Madras — A Scene in the Water –Trincomalee and Colombo—Bombay and Elephanta—The Straits of Sumatra, and the Captain's Advice — China Seas—A Typhoon — Canton—A Distinguished Naval Officer—Parting—An Historical Comparison — An Agreeable Shipmate — St. Helena—The Chops of the Channel –The Pilot Boat—A Polite Request—The Landing—Sentiment.

During this long voyage, unequalled, perhaps, in its duration since, my thoughts often reverted to my happy schooldays; and though with something of a latent, lingering desire for their return, I cannot say the comparison was detrimental to the position I then occupied. I had already imbibed a love for the profession, though the little I had seen was of a very monotonous nature; but I felt pleased with the prospect it held out of acquiring knowledge, if not distinction. My young ideas began to expand, and I contemplated the wonders of creation in the vast extent of waters, and in the magnificent brilliancy of the heavens, with an ardent imagination.

At one time I would lean over the taffrail, and gaze on the untiring, though almost imperceptible, motion of an immense shark, who followed in the wake of our ship for several days and nights, as if in expectation some accident might eventually reward his patience and perseverance, till at last he would become the victim of his own voracious nature, and gorge a hook baited with a large piece of salt pork, by which means his enormous bulk was soon laying its length on the quarterdeck. At another I would watch, with indescribable excitement and delight, the apparent evolutions of the dolphin, as, in pursuit of his prey, that would frequently fly over the ship, he would bare his golden back, and blow with his wide nostrils the spray from before him, till, after an unsuccessful chase, our men would find means to land him too on the quarterdeck; and then did I witness the truth of a description a noble poet, from his own observation, afterwards so beautifully drew of the death of that remarkable denizen of the ocean, and my memory has often been alive to the aptitude and nicety of the simile:—

"Parting day
Dies like the dolphin, whom each pang embues
With a new colour, as it gasps away
The last still loveliest—till 'tis gone, and all is gray."

At the captain's and ward-room officer's tables I listened with eager attention when the conversation turned on naval tactics or engagements, in which some one of them may have participated, and have often induced the men in the night watches to repeat some act of individual bravery, either before the enemy or in rescuing a shipmate from a watery grave. All these things, small as they may be reckoned, had entered into my system, and helped to elevate my mind far beyond my years and the sphere in which I was born. How blind are we mortals to our destiny! Who could tell that an unseen, unlooked-for agent was at work to baffle all the fond anticipations in which my boyish fancy indulged.

Though the voyage had been long, and both officers and men had suffered those privations consequent upon it, the ship was generally healthy. On the morning we dropped anchor at Kedgeree, a port on the

Hooghley, where men-of-war generally refit, but which had not been visited by a two-decked ship for nearly half a century, I was doing duty as usual in the forecastle, and, in conjunction with the boatswain, seeing the men properly stowing the jib and foretop-mast staysail. The forecastlemen had laid in, the topmen had come down from furling sails, the yards were squared, the ropes were coiled, and preparations were being made to moor the ship, when a sudden fatality befell me.

Some little time after noon I found myself laying on the armourer's chest in the gunroom, and the first person that met my eyes was a marine, who acted as the purser's servant, and through whose kindness had done me the same offices. I felt as if something had happened to me, but could not tell what. I complained of thirst, when the man gave me an orange to suck. The doctor soon after came, took hold of my hand, but said nothing. He assisted me into the purser's cabin, and laid me in his cot.

It appeared to all that I had been struck down by a *coup de solêil*, or sun-stroke, which when I was carried below was thought to be fatal, and my resuscitation did not a little surprise all hands. Without the aid of medicine I gradually recovered, and to all appearance was soon fit for duty, although from the ship's being moored, only one midshipman was necessary for each watch.

In the course of two or three days the captain went up to Calcutta, having there two brothers, one a civilian, the other in the king's or company's army. It was not long before he summoned his three youngsters to attend him there. We left the ship at midnight, not without some little apprehension, as one of our boats with six men, the coxswain and the doctor's mate, the same I have before spoken of in connection with the cobbing affair, was swamped, and every one of them had perished, it was supposed, for they were never after heard of.

Passing Saugur Island, where our ears were regaled with the yelling of tigers and the splashing of crocodiles, we arrived safely at the city of palaces, and were immediately conducted to one of them belonging to the captain's brother, who received us most hospitably, and assigned us each a bedroom, with servants to attend us.

Here we lived for about three weeks, in a most sumptuous style, attending routs and parties of the most brilliant description, and revelling in all the enjoyments of that ever gay and luxurious capital.

But the principal incident in our visit to this seat of government was our presentation, by the captain, at the levée of the governor. At that time the Marquis Wellesley held that princely office, and administered its functions with all the pomp and magnificence of an oriental ruler; at the same time, with all the grace and dignity of an accomplished English nobleman. Conducted to his presence by the captain, I was struck mute with wonder at the splendid assemblage that surrounded him — the strangeness of their colour, the richness of their costume, and the sparkling brilliancy of their jewels. On our names being announced, though before abashed and diffident, and somewhat awed in his presence, I felt relieved by the mild benignity of his manner, and could but look with admiration on this specimen of true nobility. If ever envy did possess my heart it was when that illustrious impersonation of British power and rule put his hand upon the head of my Hibernian friend and messmate, saying—

"What, is this the son of my old friend, Colonel Burgh?" and greeted him most cordially. He then expressed his pleasure at seeing us after so long a voyage, and begged we would accompany our captain to dine with him that evening. The sumptuousness of the entertainment—the quantity of gold and silver—the strange variety of the meats—the quality of the guests, and the gorgeous display that pervaded the whole scene, as it then appeared to my simple mind, far surpasses my power of description.

On the evening of our departure from this emporium of wealth and commerce, after attending another of those costly banquets, I lay down about midnight, without taking off my clothes, as the boat was to leave very early in the morning. I never knew how I reached it, for both my messmates told me it was with the greatest difficulty they awoke me; they had, indeed, almost to carry me to the waterside—this they attributed to my having indulged a little too much in the enjoyments of the table; but experience afterwards convinced me that it was a repetition of what befel me the morning we anchored at Kedgeree. However, I was perfectly recovered when we reached the ship; we found her ready for sea, and I returned to my duty as if nothing had happened.

Our next destination was Madras, to join the Admiral; and in our short passage to that Presidency we lost from sickness our only marine officer, the other being left behind at Portsmouth, as well as a midshipman, and the other doctor's mate, with two or three of the men, which we attributed to the effect of the climate upon a two-decked vessel.

We did not remain long at Madras, but long enough to witness an awful casualty, not of very frequent occurrence, but one which the sea-faring life is subject, among other dangers, unknown to the dwellers upon *terrâ firmâ.*

Whoever has been to Madras, and remained on board a ship at anchor in the roads, must know how the waters are infested with sharks, though they are seldom seen or known to rise to the surface, unless attracted by something in the shape of prey, and are therefore aptly denominated ground sharks. It was the custom to heave a studding-sail overboard in the morning, and, by attaching it to the fore and mizen chains, make a sort of pool for the men, particularly those who could not swim, to bathe in, and so preserve them from the attacks of these voracious monsters.

One of our men, an excellent swimmer, had the temerity to venture beyond the sail, when a shark like lightning rose from the bottom and with his extended jaws grasped the poor fellow's abdomen. The sea was instantly reddened with his blood; the men who were within the sail by some means rescued what was left of him from his ferocious antagonist, but life, we were all assured, was gone before we got his body on board. His mutilated remains were committed to the deep the same evening, to the great grief of his shipmates.

Some of our disrated midshipmen left us here for other ships—as did the young scion of aristocracy I have before mentioned—for England.

From thence we sailed, with the Admiral and squadron, to Trincomalee, a port on the eastern side of the island of Ceylon, and which I was told was the finest harbour in the world. I found it had not been, nor could it be, overrated ; and it presented to my view a haven possessing every advantage of security and anchorage that the most numerous fleet might require.

We were then ordered to Bombay by the Admiral, first calling at Colombo, where we took in an officer of the 19th Regiment of the Line, to do duty as marine officer; and on hearing his name I recognized an old schoolfellow from the banks of the Itchen, consequently we became on the best of terms.

Arriving at Bombay, we underwent a regular overhauling of the masts and rigging, and finding the foremast sprung two or three feet above the deck, we had to rig shears to get it out. While all hands were at work swaying up the mast, just as the heel swung clear of the deck one of the shears broke about midships, when mast, shears, and all went over the side with a tremendous crash, but without injury to any of the men, or, indeed, to any part of the ship or anything alongside.

During our stay at this presidency my time was principally occupied in going to and from the dockyard, in charge of one of the boats, either to discharge old stores, or to receive new, as we were very short of petty officers; but I managed to obtain a day to visit the cave of Elephanta, an island situate about two hours' sail from that part of the harbour of Bombay where we lay, and where are still to be seen those gigantic monuments of a bygone age, whose history, like that of our own Stonehenge, is lost in the remoteness of antiquity.

From Bombay we were ordered to proceed with convoy to China, touching at Poulon Penang, or Prince of Wales's Island. In our passage across the Bay of Bengal, and through the Straits of Sumatra, I had repeated attacks of what the doctor now decided was epilepsy, and I was ordered not to go aloft in consequence.

Becoming enervated both in body and mind, the captain one day sent for me into his cabin, and, after lamenting with much feeling the malady that had rendered me incapable of doing my duty any longer, and the little chance there appeared to be of my recovery in that climate, he said he thought he was best consulting my interest, and fulfilling the promise he had made my parents, by advising me to return to England, where I might obtain the best medical advice, and under proper care in my native land be rescued from the effects of so distressing a disorder. He then informed me that he should, therefore, on his arrival in China, seek out some homeward-bound Indiaman with whose captain he was acquainted, and procure me a passage home. To this I reluctantly, and of necessity, assented.

Proceeding on our voyage, we were overtaken in the China seas by one of those periodical storms known by the name of a Typhoon, which surpassed all I had before seen, or, indeed, have ever witnessed, at sea or on shore, in the terrific violence of its nature, and the awful appearance of the elements. Deafening claps of thunder, that seemed to threaten annihilation, instantaneously followed lightning, that, in its dart-like peculiarity of form, and unearthly variety of colour, together with the blackened intermission of its awfully vivid flash, seemed to display the vengeance of an offended Deity. The rain fell in such torrents at intervals as are only known within the tropics; while the violence of the wind agitated the waves to a degree that prevented all management of the ship.

For several hours we were under bare poles; not a stitch of canvas was to be seen in any of the fleet; the hatches were closed, and nothing but a biscuit and a glass of arrack served out to the men during the continuance of the storm, which was of thirty hours' duration.

The convoy was dispersed in all directions, owing to the violence of its effects.

The "Dedaigneuse," a small thirty-two gun frigate, rolled away, her masts under our stern, and we all expected to see her go down every minute. We afterwards learned she was saved only by the coolness, and courage, or superior seamanship of her commander—by his experience and knowledge of the proper resources in such an extremity. Our own ship rolled and pitched so unmercifully, from the short chopping nature of the sea, that it was almost impossible for the men to keep their footing, and most of them, as well as the officers, were obliged to hold on by some part of the rigging.

I myself stood on the quarter-deck grasping a rope or a belaying pin, to prevent my being tossed from one side of the ship to the other.

When the storm had abated, each ship had to make the best of her way to port; and, casting anchor at Macao, three days after we had the satisfaction of seeing our convoy pass almost singly up the river to Whampoa, nearly all in a disabled state.

A little later I accompanied the captain to Canton, and at the residence of the East India Company's agent, or consul, remained two or three days, and was introduced to the captain of a 1200 ton ship, the "Cirencester," with whom I was to take my passage to England. In their company was the captain of the "Dedaigneuse," who I soon learned was about to take his passage home in the same ship.

The captain of the Indiaman, though bred to the sea, was a gentleman of quiet manners and pleasing address, and, coming north of the Tweed, was a tolerably good specimen of a commander in the E. I. C. service.

The captain of H. M. ship "Dedaigneuse" struck me as being of a higher order. His antecedents, in regard to a very lamentable affair, had gone the round of every cockpit in the British navy for now more than a dozen years, and had surrounded his name and history with a mist, or romantic halo, in which the real character of the man was not clearly perceptible to those, who were scarcely out of their cradle, when the tragedy in which this officer played so prominent a part occurred.

Independently of the circumstances of this extraordinary tale, which were but imperfectly known to us, he was considered a very smart officer—was rich in scientific acquirements, and had already begun to give proof of them in a nautical survey of the Indian coasts, and in the construction of charts, to the great advantage of the service and the benefit of navigation. What wonder, then, that my curiosity should be excited!—or that I should seem to feel pleasure in seeing a person who had already made such a noise in the world, or rather had been so frequently of late the topic of conversation in our little circle.

I found him a man somewhat, as I thought, over five-and-thirty, a little above the middle height, attenuated in body, with every appearancc of having suffered much from the climate, fatigue, and early and long exposure to the sun; his features were regular and pleasing, his countenance, though not strongly marked or even bright, was intelligent, his eye clear, his look penetrating; but there was at that time to my idea a depression or thoughtfulness on his brow, an habitual melancholy pervading all his aspect, that told, as I thought, of bygone and severe trials.

On my introduction but few words passed between us, but enough to inspire me with a respect that requircd something more than mere rank to account for. Some conversation must have taken place between my captain and this extraordinary person before I finally found myself accompanying him on the passage home, to which I must chiefly attribute his uniform kind and friendly deportment towards me.

It was not long before I took a final leave of my shipmates, and from the manner of their farewell I had reason to believe they were sincere in their hopes of my restoration to health, and to the service. I shook each of the ward-room officers by the hand, one after the other; and fancied I saw a moisture in the eye of the plain, weather-beaten old master (Baker), with whom, for my little knowledge of navigation, I was a great favourite (he scarcely ever taking an observation without me), when he grasped my hand with both his own, and uttered his benediction on my head. The first-lieutenant, honest old Joe, as he was called, was not behind at expressing his regret at my leaving the ship; while the officer of my watch, who was more like a relative than a superior, while giving me an affectionate grasp said, he hoped on his return to England, which would not be very long first, that he should find me recovered and ready to join him in some other ship, where I might serve out my time, and then soon obtain my promotion. I replied sorrowfully, that the nature of the malady that was written on my invalid-ticket would be a bar to my ever rising in the profession—

"Stop, sir, stop!" cried the doctor, who was reclining in the after-part of the ward-room; "remember, that the greatest man that ever lived, Julius Cæsar himself, was similarly afflicted."

A smile played on my lips, though tears were in my eyes at this *jeu d'esprit*, if so it may be termed, of the doctor's, as I turned from them and made my exit.

The captain and the purser, of whom I had already taken leave, were on shore; and my chest and hammock being let down into the boat, I walked over the ship's side, not unobserved by my old friends, the captains of the forecastle and foretop, who stood waiting on the gangway, and doffing their hats begged to have the honour of shaking hands with me, as I had done with the gunner and boatswain; this I did with a full heart, and jumping into the boat had time enough to subdue my overwrought feelings before I reached the Indiaman, which had dropped down from Whampoa that morning, and to whose captain I reported myself, as his intended passenger.

The captain received me very courteously, and consigned me to the care of the third mate, who presided over the secondary portion of the officer's mess—the first and second living entirely at the captain's table; it therefore consisted of all the junior officers, and an assistant-surgeon. With these I soon made myself at home, although I had to put up with no little bantering from one or two of them, who were foremost in evincing their jealousy and dislike of his Majesty's uniform; and I had to answer to a not very polite *soubriquet*, derived from the name of the King's ship I had left.

We sailed, in company with my old ship, through the Straits of Sunda to Bencoolen, where the captain of the "Dedaigneuse" joined us. From thence we took our departure, in company with a large fleet of Indiamen, across the Indian Ocean, without convoy; and, after a good passage round the Cape, arrived safe at St. Helena.

We had not been at sea many days before the captain passenger called me on the poop, and requested me to assist him and the captain of the ship in taking a lunar observation. This I did so much to their satisfaction, that I was associated with them, in consequence of the protracted illness of the second officer, on similar occasions during the rest of the passage to England.

I must confess to having felt myself particularly flattered, as well as highly gratified, by this mark of confidence bestowed on one so young, by an officer whom my little experience assured me was much in advance of his profession; and I could but admire the unassumed gentleness of his manner, when, in casting up, or, in nautical language, working the observation and comparing the result, if there were any, the smallest, difference between us, which sometimes happened, though not frequently, he would never say I was wrong, but leave me to correct my own error, or detect his.

Thus, with the conversation I would sometimes have with this experienced and highly-intellectual naval officer, as well as noble and kind-hearted Christian, did my time pass agreeably enough, and met with no alloy from my messmates, who were in the main all good-natured fellows.

In consequence of great depredations being committed on our commerce by the French Admiral Linois, in the "Marengo," line-of-battle ship, and her companion, the "Belle Poule," a frigate that, from her sailing qualities, had bid defiance to our fastest cruisers, we were detained at St. Helena nearly three months. During that time the late captain of the "Dedaigneuse," and the only other cabin passenger, a gentleman high in office in the East India Company's Civil Service, lived entirely on shore; while I, having no money, was obliged to spend my time in the best way I could, which was principally in fishing at different points of the coast of this rocky island, where mackerel and congor-eel abound, and upon which we almost entirely subsisted — as, from the great number of ships, it was impossible to get a sufficient supply of fresh provisions from the shore; and such a surfeit did I receive of this piscatorial diet, that it was years before I could be induced to touch either of those specimens of the finny tribe.

At length H.M.S. "Athenienne,"* of sixty-four guns, arrived from England, to take charge of the largest convoy that had ever assembled at St. Helena; and after a fine passage, without meeting with anything worth recording, we arrived in the chops of the channel.

A pilot-boat coming alongside, I resolved to take advantage of it, and get on shore as quickly as I could. Accordingly I attired myself in the best my wardrobe, which had sadly diminished, would afford, and went on deck. The captain was standing on the poop, with

* This ship was in the following year lost, and the captain and all the crew perished, she having struck on a rock between Malta and Cape Pessaro, in Sicily.

his two passengers. Going up and addressing him, I said, that if he could dispense with my further services, I begged to be allowed to go on shore in the pilot-boat, as my friends lived near the coast, and I was anxious to get home, and proceeding to the Downs in the ship would take me considerably beyond it.

To this he politely gave his assent, and wished me good-bye. Turning from him, to take leave of the naval captain I have already spoken of, he took me on one side, and, casting an eye at the shabby state of my uniform, he said:—

"I am afraid you are not sufficiently prepared for any immediate expense, as, from your knocking about from port to port in India, your unexpected return, and our long stay at St. Helena, you cannot have heard from your friends, therefore take this," he added, slipping four dollars into my hand; "you can pay me when you see me, and if we do not meet I shall be no loser."

Now, considering that I had not seen the face of any coin since I left China it was not to be wondered at that I should be overcome by this act of disinterested generosity from a stranger to my family and connections. Remembering at the same time the kindness and attention I had received from one so much my superior in rank and attainments, I burst into tears; this was not unobserved by my liberal benefactor, when he again pressed my hand and bade me farewell. "Good-bye, Gramp!" hallooed the sixth mate from the port-hole, making use of the epithet by which he always addressed me, as I lowered myself down in the pilot-boat, when she almost immediately sheered off.

Now left alone on the deck, the reader would suppose I should have indulged in those pleasing anticipations that generally absorb the mind on such auspicious occasions. Not so with me; for, however I might rejoice at once more being in sight of my native land, and on the threshold, as it were, of the happy home I had left, a feeling of regret, of depression, crept over my spirits, as I felt and contemplated the farewell I had just taken of my considerate friend.

There was something about the man that attracted and commanded my respect and veneration, if not my love, independently of the interest that one awful occurrence in his early life shed round his name, the distinction he had already gained in the service, or the reputation with which his superior scientific endowments had stamped him as an ornament to his profession. Something also told me that with such an excellent specimen of humanity and myself there could be no compare—that our destinies henceforth would lay wide apart—that my malady, which had been gaining ground, would ever prevent me following in the track of so distinguished a leader, and that I must solace myself with reflecting on my good fortune in having been thrown in the path of so eminent a man.

With the scene of that farewell deeply impressed on my heart, I fell asleep, as night came on, on the deck of the pilot-boat—and, reader, it has never been effaced. It was many months —I may say two years or more—before I again fell in with my friend, and repaid him what he called the trifling obligation he had laid me under, when he took occasion to express his extreme sorrow at my having left the service.

He continued his brilliant career in the Navy till long after the revolutionary war, stimulating by his example the exertions of others, to take up, cultivate, and extend the knowledge of those branches of science that have served to raise and to adorn this noble profession. He has long since paid the debt of nature, dying at home in peace with his family, and has left behind him a name that ought to be recorded in the annals of the British Navy in letters of gold. For myself, I have ever cherished the memory of this highly gifted man, with proud delight; and looked upon the limited, though I may say familiar intercourse that passed between us, as the greatest honour I have enjoyed during my long and varied existence.*

* Captain Peter Heywood. He was accused as one of the mutineers of the "Bounty," brought to England, tried (with others of the crew) by a court-martial, assembled for that purpose on board the flag-ship at Spithead, and sentenced to death. For a full and correct account of which, together with his correspondence on that occasion, his defence, pardon, reinstatement, and continued and brilliant career in the service of his country, see "Memoirs of Peter Heywood," as compiled and published after his decease, by a near relative.

On my awaking in the morning, for I had slept soundly during the night, I found upon enquiry we were sailing up Southampton water, with a flowing tide. On reaching the quay we were not allowed to land, not having received pratique from the quarantine flag at the Motherbank, more particularly as we had a sick person on board, the second mate of the Indiaman, who had been lowered down in his cot into the pilot boat, in the last stage of consumption. Poor fellow! he breathed his last before we reached the Point at Portsmouth, where we landed after calling at the Motherbank, in preference to going back to Southampton.

When it came to my turn to get out of the boat, the master and owner of it, in a coarse rough manner, demanded my fare. Accordingly I put my hand in my pocket and presented the four Spanish dollars my kind benefactor had so generously bestowed on me, when sweeping them out of my hand, with a greedy look at them and a contemptuous one at me, he said, "You are only a poor devil of a midshipman of a man-of-war," and left me penniless to my fate.*

I set my foot on shore, and looked round me with an almost vacant mind, not at all recalling my departure from the same spot; then slowly and moodily walking up Broad Street, through Point Gates, as they were called, into the High Street, I entered one of the principal inns. Here I was much discomfited at finding myself the object of the host's studied politeness, instead of his hearty greeting as I foolishly expected.

Just at the time when I was unable to disguise my perplexity, an old female servant of my mother's coming in, recog-

* I had an opportunity a few years afterwards of recalling this gentleman to a sense of his politeness, when he called upon my father for a further loan on his vessel, upon which, at the time I speak of, the former had already advanced 300*l*.

nized me, when the tables were turned, and I received from both host and hostess a generous hospitality. From them I learned that the family were in London; and that my elder brother had left school, but was then in the town. He, on hearing from them of my sudden appearance, came and took me to my father's house.

And here, gentle reader, terminated my career on the ocean, whether for good or for ill it is not for me to say, but to bow, as I did then, to the decrees of Providence, and to agree with the philosophic bard, that "Whatever is, is right." With it ended the first stage or epoch of my life.

I returned to the bosom of my family, it is true, unsullied by the deceits, untainted by the follies, and unacquainted with the artifices of the world — uncontaminated, too, by those vices to which a sailor's life is inevitably exposed; but upon a careful retrospect I think I can descry the germ of those feelings and motives of action that afterwards brought no fruit to perfection: in other words, the impressions I received and the notions I imbibed were incompatible with success in any other sphere of life.

CHAPTER IV.

THE CHANGE.

A Coach Proprietor—Members of Parliament—A Welcome—Nelson's Funeral—The Theatres—George Frederick Cooke—John Kemble and Mrs. Siddons—The Country—A Death-bed Scene—An Elegy—The Lawyer—A Second Blow—The Wine Merchant—A Third Blow—A Valetudinarian—The Postmaster—A Scene at the Dinner-table—A Consultation and Trial—Unexpected Result—Philanthropy.

It is now necessary the reader should be informed that my father was a considerable mail contractor in the district where he lived; consequently largely embarked in the stage-coach business—a business or avocation as compatible with civic or even senatorial honours, excepting a certain desideratum, as a partnership in an extensive London brewery, or a Manchester manufacture, as subsequent events have shewn.

The first among the few coach-proprietors who ever attained this distinction stands an individual who was originally a book-keeper in one of the principal coach-offices in London.* Possessed of a dashing exterior, he managed to possess himself, by a matrimonial alliance, of considerable property; and, upon the failure of his employer, became sole proprietor of a large establishment. Connected with one stage as well as another, he contrived to insinuate himself into the favour of Richard Brinsley Sheridan, Esq., a thing not very difficult with men in affluent circumstances, and armed with a little self-importance. Accompanying him in his frequent electioneering expeditions, he became known to the electors; and, imbibing a fatal ambition, upon the death of that brilliant, but eccen-

* Richard Ironmonger, Esq., M.P. for Stafford.

tric genius, he offered himself as a candidate for the favours of the shoemakers of Stafford; and, after some few vain attempts, succeeded in being returned for that intellectual constituency. Upon one of these occasions, when he had to exhibit himself on the hustings, his speech was received with hisses and vociferations of "Off! Off!" by his opponents. Then a wag in the crowd, a friend of his own, afterwards well known to the author, slily, audibly, hallooed out, "Off with his head—so much for *Booking 'em!*" which elicited roars of laughter from both friends and foes. Poor man! he spent the greater part of his life in aping his superiors; and when he at length attained the great object of his ambition, by being, as he thought, seated beside them in the great council of the nation, death put a stop to all further aspirations, or we do not know to what office the conspicuous talent of "The frothy gentleman of Leatherhead," as he was most aptly termed, would have raised him.

Widely different was the career, as well as the attainments, of another person who issued from the same establishment, and afterwards rose first to civic, then to parliamentary honours.* Downright industry, and a systematic application to business, in which the female members of the family were called to assist, formed the foundation of his elevation. Well up in the practical part of his vocation, which he followed professionally for years, he had a very good knowledge of the animals he governed, as well as the bipeds with whom he was associated, and made them both subservient to his designs. With the employment of an oratory he could at all times most powerfully use, though it was not adapted to the

* William T. Chaplin, Esq., late M.P. for Salisbury.

atmosphere of St. Stephen's, he added an intellect superior to most of his class in shrewdness and tact, and this with a soft oily expression, that procured for him the soubriquet of "Bite 'em sly." He possessed, also, a sort of playful sarcasm, he was fond of exhibiting, under which he disguised his real object; by these gifts he raised himself to eminence, and procured a host of worshippers.

There were others who rose from the most menial situations, compared with these, to be members of the same august body. With wits sharpened in the lowest purlieus of an inn, they acquired in the north an habitual taste for railway transactions; and when the mania was at its zenith, they snatched the opportunity of gaining a position, that gave them such an amount of patronage, as would at any time ensure their election for small constituencies, such as Salisbury, York, Bodmin, Harwich, and similar places.

" 'Tis success that colours all in life:
Success makes fools admired and villains honest.
All the vain pomp and glory of the world
Wait on success and power, howe'er acquired."

At the time of my coming home from sea my father was in London, where he had purchased a very large establishment in his own line of business, at the cost of several thousands of pounds, of the frothy gentleman before spoken of; leaving my elder brother to superintend the business in the country; but he did not long remain there. He very injudiciously, as it appeared, took in as a partner the man who had not long before failed there;* and he, to the best of my memory, took the first opportunity of getting out without any material loss. Better had it been for himself and his family if he had never returned to it, which he unfortunately did some few years afterwards. But let me not anticipate.

The morning after my landing at

* The late George Boulton.

Portsmouth, I was sent off to London; and arriving in the evening, my father met me, and took me to his residence in the immediate neighbourhood. I shall not attempt to describe the emotions of my heart at once more being embraced by a fond and excellent mother, as well as by my elder sister, who had been my principal correspondent, and had been attentive to all my requests. I remained in town during the winter, almost daily visiting either Guy's or St. Thomas's Hospital, but my malady was at length deemed incurable. Consequently, my invalid-ticket was exchanged for a discharge from the Royal Navy, as I was considered, from the state of my health, incapable of serving his Majesty. My father, not satisfied with this, took me to more than one eminent physician, all, however, with the same result. Indeed, my malady seemed to set all medical aid at defiance, and it was thought best to let it take its course.

During my residence in London, the funeral of the great Nelson took place; and I may here mention, that my father was the last person who shook hands with the illustrious hero on English ground, having accompanied him to the Sallyport, and held an umbrella over his head, on his embarcation from Portsmouth, prior to the fatal battle of Trafalgar. I had, with some friends of the family, who had procured tickets, seen the body lay in state at Whitehall, and afterwards stood upon one of the sides of the arch of Temple Bar, as the procession passed under.

I also frequented the theatres and other places of amusement; my father being intimate with the proprietor of Covent Garden, and holding shares himself in Drury Lane, I had many opportunities of witnessing the performances of those celebrated artists, Cooke, J. Kemble, and Mrs. Siddons, in, I may say, all their principal characters. Their inimitable representations put all other pretenders in the shade, while the dramatic hemisphere was illumined by the splendour of their talents.

I remember about this time to have met, more than once or twice, the great George Frederick Cooke (for great he was in his profession), at a dinner-party in London, in company with my parents,* and had an opportunity of observing in private, the most prominent characteristics of that deservedly popular, though somewhat eccentric, actor. In person he was inclined to be tall and athletic (on the stage his figure was majestic), with a countenance not handsome, at the same time not unpleasing, for there was a good-natured smile lurking at each corner of his mouth; while his large, dilating eye sparkled with hilarity, even in his most sober moments; but which ex-

* See "Memoirs of George Frederick Cooke," by Dunlop, first published in the United States.

pression he could quickly change into one of angry dispute or grave discussion, should offensive personality provoke the one, or serious reasoning invite the other; indeed, sometimes his countenance would assume a malevolence of expression I have rarely, if ever, seen surpassed.

In conversation, while sober, and I never saw him otherwise in the company of ladies, he was fluent if not eloquent —his manners bland if not polished—rich in anecdote, acute of understanding, bright and quick in *repartée*, slow but severe in his satire, generally just though approaching to sarcasm in his observations, and conveying to the youthful mind a fund of pleasing intelligence.

Indeed, I fancied I could discern in his strongly-marked features, the wicked dissimulation, the unscrupulous ambition, and the princely dignity of *Richard*, the implacable hatred of *Shylock*, the malicious cunning of *Iago*, the worldly accomplishments of *Sir Pertinax*, and the comic irony of *Falstaff*. In all these characters he was not to be equalled; in one part only, in that of *Sir Giles Overreach*, in Massinger's play of a "New Way to Pay Old Debts," did I ever afterwards think that a versatile professor of the histrionic art, upon whom his mantle was made to fall,* come up to the delineations of this consummate actor. What a pity it is that such lofty gifts should have been marred by the most vulgar of vices!

It may be considered foreign to the subject, but I cannot quit this part of my life without recording my equal admiration of his more classic rival, more particularly in his Roman characters; and my youthful, and afterwards my more matured adoration of his illustrious sister.

* It was generally reported, that at the time of the introduction of the elder Kean to a London audience, an assemblage of the principal proprietors and editors of the London papers took place at Holland House to favour his reception; but I cannot state it as a fact.

Some actors, it must be acknowledged, have put forward pretensions to emulate the performance of the two former — the latter stood alone and remained unrivalled. Shakespere's *Lady Macbeth* and Mrs. Siddons have gone to the grave together.

After spending some months in London, without any benefit to my still declining health, I was sent to my father's residence in the country, where I spent my time principally in reading; for I had begun to acquire sedentary habits. Sometimes I employed myself in gardening; at others, I was induced to accompany an affectionate sister in rambling over the neighbouring downs, and often in gossiping with and listening to the tales of the villagers; one of whom, I remember, was an old smuggler, who would amuse me with accounts of his feats of courage, or of cunning—telling

> " Of most disastrous chances,
> Of moving accidents by flood and field,
> Of hair-breadth 'scapes;"

Following no occupation, I became idle and listless.

Suddenly I was called away to the Isle of Wight, to attend the dying bed of my elder brother. I have not passed through a long life without having been much subjected to these sorrowful visitations of Providence: in every relation of life, as a son, a brother, a husband, a father, have I had to bow to the decrees of the Almighty, and with becoming fortitude and resignation bear the grief inflicted by His chastening rod; but this was the first, and it is not to be wondered at, if it made a deep and lasting impression on my then youthful heart.

The shock which the mind receives from the death of a near and dear relative, cut off in the bloom of health and pride of youth, makes it loth to surrender its grief, even to the growing incidents and allurements that time may throw in the way, particularly where there is little else to dwell on.

He was a fine handsome promising youth, in his eighteenth year, endeared to the family circle by a most amiable disposition, and, by his manly and generous conduct, had won the admiration and enjoyed the friendship of many persons of his own age and station. He was on an excursion of pleasure round the Island, with two or three others, prior to their entering on their studies necessary for the profession each of them had adopted. He was a most excellent swimmer, but imprudently, without a thought of the consequences, under a noonday's sun in the autumn, undressed after a long ride on horseback, and plunged into the sea, to indulge in his favourite pastime.

How he was first taken I do not know; but I found him in a cottage at Shanklin, in bed, with a burning fever—attended by our weeping parents and our elder sister—which, in a few days, proved fatal.

This was a severe blow to all, though I remember my sister then first manifested that spiritual endowment which she has had occasion to exercise in so many similar instances, and which has earned for her the enduring love and esteem of her numerous relatives. My brother's remains were interred in a vault my father had built for the purpose, in our parish church of Catherington, and were attended to their last resting-place by his sorrowing relatives and his most intimate companions.

On the Sunday following, I remember, a most impressive discourse was delivered by the parochial minister,* whose eloquence not only reached the heart of those nearly allied to him, but drew tears from the eyes of the rustic congregation.

The following lines, written by one pre-

* The Rev. G. G. Griffinhoof.

sent on that solemn occasion, and afterwards sent to my elder sister, will give some idea of the loss we all sustained, and at the same time do credit to the writer's mind and heart as an elegiac production :—

LINES WRITTEN BY EDWARD BINSTEAD,

A FRIEND AND COMPANION OF THE LATE ——, WHO WAS A WITNESS TO HIS END, AND AGAINST WHOM INJURIOUS REPORTS HAD BEEN FALSELY CIRCULATED.

WHILE sad remembrance paints the scene of woe,
My tortur'd breast its anguish will reveal;
In spite of consolation tears will flow,
And silent tell the poignant grief I feel.

Scarce had he to meridian beauty rose,
When, in a sudden and eventful hour,
He sunk eternal to that long repose
Where mortals all must yield their boastful pow'r.

'Twas then that calumny, with poison'd breath,
To malice lent her pestilential aid,
And falsely said that in his lingering death
That friendship, inhumanity betray'd.

Ah! who can feel his grievous loss more dear,
Or at his melancholy fate repine?
Friends of his youth might drop a genuine tear,
But all their sorrows cannot equal mine.

For may I not superior sorrow claim,
Who knew his worth, and saw the pains he bore?
Parental woe might know a pang the same,
But e'en their misery cannot feel it more.

Intrusive thought! why wilt thou piercing steal
To paint the hapless day that snatch'd him hence?
Reflections here a train of woes reveal,
And grief's increas'd by funeral eloquence.

Not all the ills that sympathy had taught
That solemn scene, when to the hallow'd shrine
I follow'd him: not then such grief had brought
As that inflicted by the good Divine.

Each village rustic felt its solemn force,
For each had known the virtues of his mind;
Affliction's tear fell from its native source,
And all the neighbouring train in sorrow join'd.

Pensive where rest his ashes will I stray,
When evening spreads its melancholy gloom
And through the village churchyard bend my way,
To heave the sigh of sorrow o'er his tomb.

Not long after this visitation of Providence it was thought necessary that I should follow some profession; and my father, observing my studious disposition, articled me to an attorney. The person selected for my governor, or instructor, in this, what ought to be, honourable profession, was a plain, plodding country lawyer, of good family and connections, in excellent repute as a conveyancer, and, what is more rare, a man of probity and honour, to whom many of the neighbouring gentry committed the management of their affairs, and whose general practice did not descend to take part in those disputes that, arising from the frailties, the vices, or the misfortunes of mankind, give employment to the talents and virtues of the greater part of the practitioners in what is termed Common Law.

He was also a man of an equable temper, not easily provoked, of a kind and friendly disposition, devoted to his family, and a most lenient master. He had, I remember, an excellent library, in which I used to spend my time, out of, and frequently in, office-hours; for there was more attraction for me in the perusal of our English classics, particularly Dryden and Pope, than in studying the dry disquisitions of Hale, Coke, or Blackstone.

But my progress, whether slow or

otherwise, was suddenly cut short. My governor having stepped out for a few minutes while the other clerks had gone to their dinner, and leaving me alone in the office, on his return found me in one of the dreadful fits that had so long afflicted me; and what made it worse, I was attacked so near the fire, that, had he not returned as he did, I must have been burned to death; as it is, I carry the scars of the wounds about me I received on that occasion to this day.

This had such an effect on the nerves of the good man, that he requested my father to take me home, as he dreaded the responsibility he had incurred by taking charge of one in so precarious a state of health, and most honourably returned the very considerable premium my father had paid with me.

I cannot say I felt any regret at leaving, for I had no fondness for the profession, and my malady had already began to make me indifferent to any constant employment.

Accordingly I was taken home—but not to our house in the country—again to spend my time in idleness; for soon after, or about this time, my father had—for what cause I know not, except with a view to provide for me—embarked largely in the wine trade. Importations were made from Oporto, Cadiz, and other foreign marts; and the large cellar of our house in the High Street was well stored with wines of every description, and of the choicest vintage; for my father was considered an excellent judge, and had good connections both in the army and navy. The whole was committed to the care of an experienced cellarman, long known to the family, to whose charge, as regarded my health, and a watchful observation of my movements, I was also consigned.

Everything went on well for some little time, and a good trade had already been established, when one day I was down in the cellar superintending — or, rather, in company with the man, for I could only look on — the bottling off a pipe of port. The cask had been drawn off, the bottles arranged in regular order ready for corking, when suddenly, without the smallest notice, I fell crash among the bottles, breaking and destroying a considerable number, and lacerating my hands and face awfully with the fragments, till the floor of the cellar was absolutely flooded with the generous liquor, not unmixed with some few drops of what was more precious to me, and the loss of which added not a little to my already weakened state and now woeful appearance.

On the arrival from the country of my father, who was speedily made acquainted with what had occurred, the cellars were closed, and in a few days the whole genuine stock of wines was offered for sale. They were eagerly purchased by an old-established wine-merchant in the town, who was glad to get rid of a formidable rival to the monopoly on which my father had already committed a great inroad.

After that calamity all thoughts of my ever being fit for any profession or employment were abandoned, and I was kept at home, under the watchful care of one or other of the family, who never suffered me to go out of his sight. I now became sensible that I was a burden to those about me, although the most constant and tender attention was bestowed on my every movement—indeed on my every look; and I was fully alive to and grateful for this affectionate solicitude. But my spirits sunk with my health; and, giving up all hopes of partaking in the enjoyments of youth either mentally or bodily, and losing all inclination for society, I acquired a silent and melancholy manner.

It was early in the year 1807 that a new postmaster was appointed at Portsmouth, in consequence of the death or superannuation of one who had grown old in the service. An office of such considerable importance and responsibility—consequently one of good emolument—was bestowed on a gentleman closely connected with the Baronet (Sir Francis Freeling) who so long and so efficiently fulfilled the office of Secretary to the Postmaster-General. He had not long taken possession of his new appointment before my father called on him, as it was quite necessary, from the relative situation he stood in with the Post-Office as Mail Contractor, that they should be known to each other, if not be on friendly terms. This induced a reciprocity of visits; and my father, with his accustomed hospitality, took an early opportunity of inviting him and his family to dinner. They accordingly came, and, while seated at the table, the whole party were suddenly discomfited by an attack of my fearful enemy—for fearful were the distortions of my countenance in all such lamentable visitations. I was borne to my room, and did not again make my appearance that evening; but I understood that I and my dreadful malady formed the topic of conversation in my absence. Indeed, on my recovery, my sister told me that the gentleman had evinced great commiseration for my affliction; and in the course of conversation, after asking many questions as to its general nature and origin, said he was acquainted with a person in London who he was sure could cure me.

This drew a smile of sorrowful incredulity from the lips of my father, who, after having sought and had the best advice the most celebrated of the faculty could afford, had no faith in the ability of any unknown doctor or acknowledged empiric

My mother was not so disinclined, but listened with avidity to the many instances of successful trials our new acquaintance cited, and upon which he founded his conviction that, were I to take his friend's specific, I should at no very distant date be restored to health. In the morning he called to ask after me, and again took an opportunity of imploring my parents to try the remedy he had named, or, at least, to allow him to write to the person to ask his opinion of my case. He then appealed to me, who had long despaired of any remedy, and I avowed that I should do exactly as my parents wished, but gave him to understand I should have no faith whatever in any medicine his friend or any one else might prescribe—at the same time kindly thanking him for the interest he had evinced for me.

At length, after frequent importunities, he prevailed and obtained both my father's and mother's permission to write the particulars of my case to the gentleman he had named.

In due time an answer came to say that he had considered my affliction, and had not the least doubt that, with the aid of the Almighty, if I persevered and took the medicine which he from time to time would send me, I should eventually be restored. This, he said, might not occur till after an interval of three, six, or nine months, and we were not to be alarmed if my fits became more frequent and lasted longer. He assured us that eventually they would quite leave me, and a permanent cure be effected.

I commenced taking the medicine early in February. The professional gentleman who had attended our family for many years—a man of good understanding and extensive practice—on his first visit put his tongue to the liquid, which was of a most nauseous nature, shook his head in ignorance of its qualities, but said not a word to discourage us in the trial of it. . ...

The spring had passed away, and the summer brought with it an aggravation of my malady—that is, my fits had become much more frequent, and the convulsions of longer duration; so much so, that the family became alarmed, and our medical man, who had watched its effects and began to fear the worst, advised us to discontinue following the prescription.

Accordingly a letter was written to that effect, to which an answer was returned (and which is now in my possession), urging me to keep on with the medicine, stating that the result hitherto was no more than he had predicted, and quoting a similar case, where, under similar circumstances, it had recently proved successful.

A long discussion now took place, and various and contradictory were the opinions given. The gentleman who had first recommended the trial, and had since shewn a keen interest in its progress, having every faith in his friend's panacea, urged its continuance—my mother doubted, while my father, the medical man, and my late instructor in the law, who happened to be present, and had not ceased, nor ever did cease, to take a lively interest in my welfare, said it had better be given up.

At last it was determined to leave it to myself; while I, having been some time convinced that it was a desperate remedy, and feeling that life with the prospect of an impaired intellect would not be worth possessing, decided instantly on going on with the medicine. This was in July. Another month had scarce elapsed when a day passed over the time in which I was usually attacked—then another, and another. My sister and my mother looked at each other with surprise, not daring to express the hopes that had begun to possess their minds.

A week passed without my being at all affected, and it was thought advisable to apprise the gentleman in London of so favourable an occurrence. To this no reply was received; consequently, at the end of the second week another letter was despatched, stating that I still remained free from any further attack of my late distressing visitor, and begging to know if I were to continue the medicine.

On the 9th of September a letter was received, which announced my cure; and from that time to this I have enjoyed, through the blessing of Providence, almost uninterrupted good health. It is but justice to add, that this gentleman, (whom I never saw, for he died a short time after,) in his letter congratulated me on my recovery, but took no credit to himself, and impressed on me how much I was indebted to the goodness of God, who had made him the means to rescue me from that idiotcy to which I was fast approaching, and for which I never could be too grateful.

Upon being applied to for his charge, he some time afterward enclosed the apothecary's bill, amounting to 15*l.* only, and stated that he was satisfied in being the instrument whereby such good had been done to his fellow-creatures. An instance of true philanthropy, of rare occurrence, and I think worth recording: although the logic made use of by those of the faculty, who at the time derided the means of cure, as well as other practitioners of the present day, who deny the existence of the malady in my case,—may not be.

CHAPTER V.

EARLY LIFE.

Convalescence—Thoughts for the Future—The Sixth Mate —Amusements—A Rash Adventure—A Literary Society —Junius—Lord Macaulay—A Character—A Fire—Gunpowder Companionship—Lord Gambier—Sir Eliab Harvey—Sir Roger Curtis—Lord Cochrane—A Curious Rencontre—The Prince of Wales—A Dreadful Explosion—Wonderful Escape—A Rash Attempt.

Emerging from this long course of sickness and despondency, I did not, as many would suppose, immediately mix in the affairs of the world—its pleasures, its business, its allurements, or its follies. It took some time to renovate my strength. My constitution, which must have been sadly torn and weakened by such repeated violent attacks, required care and attention to restore me to anything like convalescence, and to enable me, both in body and mind, to become a member of society at all. Consequently, a year passed away before I sought any companions, or followed any business.

During this time many were the projects thought of, and plans laid out, for my future. The first question mooted was, would I go back to the profession I was so fond of, and in the scientific part of which I had made so much progress? Alas! that had all vanished, as well as other acquirements, owing partly to the want of practice, and partly — indeed chiefly—to the malady, that had so affected my brain as to deprive it almost of the power of retention, and to dissipate the fruits of early application, and fair natural capabilities.

To this return I clung with an eager tenacity, although with groundless hope, till learning from a high quarter that, having received my discharge, the time I had already served would not be allowed when I should attempt to pass for a lieutenant, the idea was abandoned; and the gentleman, who had some interest at the Admiralty, and had kindly exerted it for me, observing my predilection for the Navy, offered to procure me a commission in the Royal Marines. But I had, as a midshipman, foolishly imbibed the dislike to that corps that had long existed in the cockpit; therefore, I immediately declined the offer.

Would I go back to the law? My vacancy had long been filled up, and I could fancy no other master—neither had I any affection for the profession. Another thing, and that which mainly contributed to my remaining at home, was the loss of my elder brother. I had now become the eldest son; consequently my parents did not promote any plan that would require a long absence, or expose me to the risk of any return of my recent affliction.

Thus, then, did another twelvemonth of my life pass away, the monotony of which was now and then relieved by the visits of some early friends of my father; among others an old-fashioned gentleman from Cambridge, I remember, with his daughter and son. The latter had just then been appointed to the command of a sloop-of-war, and ever afterwards made our house his home when his ship came into port. I also saw some relatives of my mother's; and once my home was enlivened by a short visit from my old friend the sixth mate, who amused our family circle with his quaint expressions, and his bluff, sailor-like manner—for, though a rough diamond, he was a genuine, straight-forward fellow, and had always possessed my regard. He was at that time second officer of the H.E.I.C. ship the "Elphinstone," and boasted of having gone round the Cape twelve times outward and homeward without carrying away a spar—so little danger was there in a life at sea. Poor fellow!—he at last got killed by the natives in the Straits of Malacca, when going on shore for wood.

Advancing to manhood, it is not to be supposed that I was free from those little indiscretions to which youth is prone, nor is it necessary to particularize them. It may be enough to acknowledge that, in the language of the present day, I might be considered rather a fast young man. Being, as it were, the representative of my father, who held a respectable position in the town, and having the management or superintendence of an extensive concern confided to me, I had a liberal allowance, and a good horse to ride; this was the more necessary, as I had to visit the different stages where the horses stood. Such out-door exercise proved beneficial to my health, so that I began to shake off all effects or fear of my late malady. Among other things, I joined a cricket-club, principally composed of officers in the garrison—this was the means of my introduction to a new and wide field of acquaintance; and then I partook of, and entered with spirit into, all the manly sports and pastimes then in vogue, including cock-fighting and bull-baiting, which had not then been abandoned.

I also joined the Yeomanry Cavalry, at that time commanded by a son of the East India Company's agent at Portsmouth; * and as I had the means of mounting my principal clerk as one of the troop, and my foreman in the stables as a trumpeter, I was pretty well recommended to the notice of the Colonel-commanding and the Adjutant, the latter being an intimate friend of our family. These avocations extended my acquaintance among some of the most flourishing

* John Lindegren, Esq.

tradesmen in the town, as well as the leading farmers and dealers in the country. Among the former was a man some few years older than myself, who was the sergeant-major, and a very efficient soldier he was; being a good swordsman, as well as a most excellent horseman.

Of these qualities he had given me a proof, which was the cause, if not the commencement, of our friendship. Being in London for the first time since my recovery, I determined to see the Derby, for which purpose I borrowed a nag from a well-known horse-dealer in London, with whom my father was acquainted. The animal on which I was mounted threw me three times between Bethlem Hospital and Epsom, and was altogether a restive and unruly brute. Meeting the serjeant-major on the Downs, with an intimate friend of mine in a gig, they observed by the dust on my coat that I must have had a fall; on my telling them how I had been served, he volunteered to ride the mare home, while I should take his place by the side of my friend; to this I readily assented, and aided by a heavier weight and a stronger nerve, which his confidence as a rough rider gave him, he took the mare safe to her owner's stables.

He was also of a gay and convivial disposition, and our inspections and field-days on Portsdown-hill were sometimes wound up with a good feed, and an evening devoted to a rather tumultuary sacrifice to Bacchus. But this would only happen when we dined *en troupe;* on other occasions, after being dismissed, we would ride home together in small parties, each selecting his own fancy "Public" on the road for refreshment or enjoyment. Generally I found myself side by side with this sergeant-major, for he was a congenial spirit, and we were associates in many a pleasurable gathering in the Isle of Wight—always a favourite spot of mine, in consequence of the genuine hospitality I received from many of its inhabitants—where business and pleasure frequently led my friend. One day after drill, we took our chop at the principal house in the village of Cosham, substituting brandy-and-water for the more genteel and customary bottle of old port. This was a beverage I was then but little acquainted with; however, we mounted at dusk, to ride gently and quietly home.

We had proceeded in friendly chat uninterrupted about half way, when I heard the sound of music; and as we approached the house or inn from which the dulcet notes proceeded, we discerned by the lights a large party of both sexes tripping it on the light fantastic toe, in a lofty room in rear of, and partly over the bar, the access to which was by wooden steps from the road. Without a moment's thought of the danger or the consequences, whether instigated by the rather unusual quantity of spirits I had taken with my pipe, or prompted by an innate love of mischief, I, without checking her, guided my high-spirited but well-trained black mare up the steps and in at the door. My friend, at all times ready for what is now vulgarly called a lark, followed me; and there we sat, erect in our saddles, our swords drawn, and our pistols in the holsters, to the amazement and consternation of the whole party.

After the screaming of the softer sex and the uproarious laughter of the other, which so foolish an exhibition had at first elicited, had somewhat subsided, our first consideration—for we had none before—was how to beat a retreat from an assembly whose numbers were overpowering, and whose merriment, I begun to suspect, might speedily be changed into anger at our rash and indecent intrusion. The company consisted chiefly of dockyard mechanics, "their sweethearts and spouses," always a formidable body, and ready to resent any such impudent and outrageous innovation on their evening's amusement.

Nevertheless, preserving my presence of mind, I very deliberately dismounted, and taking hold of the mare's bridle, with a soldier's step, caused her to keep pace with me down the rude and ruinous staircase we had but a few minutes before recklessly ascended. The sergeant-major following my example, was equally successful in gaining the road in safety, and our dangerous frolic ended in treating the whole assembly with sundry bowls of punch (we were none of us niggards on such occasions), which seemed to allay the pugnacious spirit of some of the party, who had evinced a strong inclination to bestow on us that sort of punishment our mad attempt at fun had so richly deserved; and this perhaps was in a great measure prevented by the superior tact and determination of my companion, who personally knew several of the men. As if to aggravate my offence, standing in the crowded bar, my spurs and sword became entangled in some choice dresses that lay in one corner on the floor after a day's bleaching, which roused the indignation of the landlady; and no doubt a summary ejectment would have been effected had I not hastily made my escape, mounted, and rode off. The sergeant-major soon followed and over-took me, and after congratulating each other on the result of so foolish an adventure, we said "good night."

On the following morning I called and made my peace with the landlady, by liberally paying her demand for all damages sustained.*

But with all this, I sought and kept good society. The family living almost entirely in the country, I had many leisure hours to dispose of; and preferring the company of my elders and men of good position in the town to those of my own age, I was induced to make one to join —indeed to found—a literary society,

* On a recent excursion for the benefit of my health, I by chance entered an inn in a market-town in Sussex. A gentleman, with hoary locks like myself, sitting with a pint of wine before him, attracted my attention. I felt convinced I had seen him before, and, after strictly scrutinizing his features, I recognized my old friend the sergeant-major, although I had seen him but once in forty years. Addressing him rather abruptly, I said, "If ever I saw E. G. I see him now!" He rose from his seat, and said, "You are right, sir, but I have no recollection of you." I asked him if he was not once a non-commissioned officer in the Hants Yeomanry Cavalry. He said, certainly. I then recalled this incident to his memory; he instantly grasped my hand, and, shaking his head at the same time, said, "Now I know you, for none but T. C. would have led the way; and I never pass the house," he added, "without a vivid recollection of all the circumstances, and the danger we were in, as well from the crazy state of the building as from our wanton indiscretion."

after the manner of the one mentioned by Benjamin Franklin. We were in number about seven or eight, all married men but myself, and I was at that time under twenty years of age. It was our custom to meet every Monday evening, at the house of one of our members, who possessed an extensive library. The chair was taken by rotation, and the president elect would name the subject for discussion on the ensuing night of meeting—thus giving us all time to study it, and to form our opinions upon it, which we delivered *extempore*, or from a written paper, as we chose. The discussion ended, and our different opinions recorded in a journal kept for that purpose—which journal, by-the-bye, is now in existence—the president would read something of his own selection, either in prose or verse, from the best English authors, generally in accordance with the subject we had been debating.

I look back with no small degree of satisfaction at this part of my younger days, as it was not time ill spent—indeed, the employment was both rational and instructive; and I have lived to see institutions much resembling our little society grow up in many of our populous towns and districts. It tended also to improve those faculties with which the Almighty had endowed us; and if not of practical utility in every-day life, it strengthened our sphere of knowledge; with me in particular, it helped to invigorate the mind, and to re-instate it in its former fondness for literature.

I remember about this time a weekly paper was published in London, called the *Independent Whig*. Its name alone was indicative of its politics, and in its attacks upon the Government it went much further than any other publication, Cobbet's *Register* not excepted. As I often found time to stroll into a bookseller's shop to read the

London papers, the proprietor of which was one of the "L. S.," as we were called, *par excellence*, I used frequently to see this paper, and was more than once struck with the great similarity there appeared in the style of its leading articles (if the large type in the first page may be so termed) and the letters of Junius; and when I read the one that contained so severe an attack on the Duke of Cumberland, and stated that H.M. King George the Third would shortly be called upon to perform the part of a Roman father, I was assured of the identity. It was generally understood at that time that Sir Philip Francis, then an old man, and living in St. James's Square, was a contributor to the *Independent Whig*; and Mr., subsequently Lord Macaulay, has since endeavoured to prove that he was the author of Junius. In proposing this for discussion at our little society, I could not get any one to listen to my conclusions; as, in the first place, I was not yet sufficiently qualified to judge of style, after comparing one with the other; and, in the second, they all asserted and agreed that the author of Junius had been dead many years. Although I could not give any further evidence in favour of his identity, I could not be diverted from that opinion—an opinion which I ever after maintained, and which I see confirmed by the first critic and historian of the age.

I shall not attempt to give a description of each individual member of our little institution, but shall say at once they were all men of intellect and education, well known in their different vocations, and commanded, or rather held, a highly respectable position among the community of which they formed a part; nevertheless, I cannot refrain from drawing an outline of one, to whom I was particularly attached, who was the original projector, as well as the hospitable owner of the house where our meetings were held — of one who afterwards attained to some distinction, and rendered considerable service to the Government in the Colonies, and one of whom it may be justly said that, for many excellent qualities, "we shall not look upon his like again."

He was in person above the common size, tall and stout, well-made and strongly knit, his figure, without being graceful, exhibiting great bodily strength and activity. Nature had endowed him with an excellent constitution, and great powers of endurance. Few could come up to him in walking, running, jumping, skating, or any commonly practised gymnastics. His countenance was in unison with his frame; for, without being handsome, it was expressive of quick determination and manly resolution; while his full, piercing gray eye, gleaming from an iron complexion, surmounted by dark, crisp, curly locks, denoted a temper perhaps more vehement than ductile; in a word, he had all the *fortiter in re*, without that admixture of the *suaviter in modo*, necessary to make what is called an amiable man.

"I do not know what this young man means," said Sylla, putting his hand upon the head of Cæsar; "but what he means he does with vehemence."*

And this characteristic, if small *men* may be compared with great, may justly be applied to my friend. His manners were not so engaging as they were open and ingenuous. In conversation, he was more dictatorial than agreeable; in argument, more dogmatic than convincing; and yet was not impatient of contradiction, and would yield like a lamb to what he had contested for like a lion, when he found his position no longer tenable; and, generally speaking, his in-

* Plutarch's "Life of Julius Cæsar."

formation upon most matters was good, and his observation just.

He had an excellent taste for literature, though it partook more of the grave and instructive than the polite and amusing. He had also imbibed a strong predilection for the sweets of gastronomy, which gave a zest to his hospitality; and, among those who knew him, did not detract from the pleasures of the table—in short, he had all the peculiarities of a thorough-bred Englishman; and one of his particular though perhaps not the wisest of his maxims was, that nothing should be done—no houses or acres bought and sold — no bargain made — no election, whether of mayor, members of Parliament, or churchwarden — no meeting, without a good dinner. With all this he was a man of sterling merit, strict integrity, undoubted truthfulness, uncompromising rectitude, sturdy independence, and strong, natural good feeling towards his fellow-creatures.

He possessed a fair share of oratory; could express himself with energy and eloquence, if not with brilliancy; was of sound understanding, well read in history, more particularly that of his own country, her laws and institutions. He was of inflexible purpose, not easily daunted; but doing all that became a man when circumstances rendered a decided action necessary.

As an instance of individual bravery I may mention, that one evening, nearly at the termination of our meeting, we were suddenly aroused from our discussion by the cry of "fire!" proceeding from the street. We all immediately rushed to the front-door, when we found a large ironmonger's shop and house, a few doors down the street, on the opposite side of the way, becoming a prey to the ravages of the flames, which were fast issuing from the windows of the first and second floors. We had not stood long gazing at the fire, before an alarm ran through the crowd that there was gunpowder in the house; and one of the assistants in the shop came and whispered the fact to my friend, who, having ascertained in what part of the house it was deposited, and the quantity, immediately cried out, with a stentorian voice—for that was a gift dame nature had liberally bestowed on him—

"Will any man go up with me, and bring the powder down?"

I was standing by his side, and felt as if the challenge was meant for me; but my heart sunk within me as I contemplated the little chance of success. A few seconds only elapsed before a corporal of marines, who stood a few yards from us, responded, "I will, sir!" and came forward.

"Don't—pray, don't!" said I to the first;

and his other friends, taking hold of his arm, implored him not to rush into such imminent peril. He shook us off, and, followed by the soldier, he was seen to enter the house by the private door, and heard ascending the staircase. A breathless silence pervaded the crowd, which now amounted to between two and three thousand. Those who were at work at the engines stopped, and stood in the attitude of fearful expectation—all waiting the result with the most intense anxiety. Those who anticipated the explosion held their breath with fear, while some few whispered a prayer for the safety of the two who had so hopelessly rushed into danger. As for me, I looked round to the house we had just left, where dwelt his wife and two sweet children, and could think of nothing but the mournful fate that awaited them; when suddenly, after a fearful absence, a loud hurrah announced that they had issued safely from the house, each bearing on his head a cask of gunpowder. These they carried safely to the guard-house, distant about sixty or seventy yards, and there left in charge of the officer on duty; and then they returned to receive the cheers and congratulations of the crowd on the success of their hazardous enterprize.

The engines now played with redoubled force, the fire was soon subdued, and its ravages confined to that one house.

This exemplary act of courage, showing a disregard of danger when a great calamity was impending, raised him very much in the estimation of the whole community, and he long held a commanding influence in the town; for he could at all times raise or control the *vox populi*, whether at a political meeting, or any other public occasion—such as a day set aside for rural sports and rejoicings, in which all classes would join, and of which he always took the direction.

I have been thus prolix in a tribute of respect to one of my early friends, as I consider his merits and qualifications would have done honour to a higher sphere than that in which his lot was cast. He still lives in the author's friendship and esteem, and may be seen in London, after a long, toilsome, but to him not weary pilgrimage, wending his way with a slow, somewhat altered, but not yet crippled gait, towards the British Museum; or seated in the splendid library of that magnificent establishment; as upright in his stature as in his mind, waiting with the same undaunted spirit—and, it is to be hoped, with that humble reliance on the merits and mediation of One who took our nature upon him, and died for us all—that fiat that must shortly remove him "to another and a better world."

With this friend was I associated in everything that was worthy of observation, and with every occurrence of importance, in the naval and military departments. Was there a ship-launch in the dockyard, we were there; was a line-of-battle ship—a first-rate—going out of or coming into harbour, we were on the platform to witness the magnificent spectacle; was there a regiment of the line about to march down the High Street to the Sally-port, to embark for foreign service, we were sure to meet them at the Landport-gates, and accompany them, keeping time to their martial music; did a detachment of invalids, sick or wounded, disembark, we were on the beach to receive them; did a bull-bait take place in the neighbourhood, or a cock-fight call us out of town, we were there too. Of the first, I may say I never witnessed but one; but the picture of the maddened beast, the sleek and courageous dog tossed high in the air—

his master, running with outstretched arms to catch him—while his entrails protruded from the orifice made by the horns of the foaming and bellowing bull, the tears of anguish shed over his pet friend and companion by the man who had trained him to the cruel sport, of which he had just become the victim, convinced us both that it was a most degrading pastime. The other, though of an equally demoralizing nature, did not appear as brutal in its character, and did not attract such low company.

There was a gentleman in the little town of Bishops Waltham that annually had an exhibition of this sort, who generally had some first-rate birds, and we were in the habit of meeting there some of the first people in the neighbourhood.

On one of these occasions I remember two men, who had the appearance of gentlemen, but were nothing more than

London black-legs, as was afterwards ascertained. They refused to pay some bets I had fairly won of them, so I unceremoniously horsewhipped them out of the pit.

But from these peccadilloes of a youthful spirit, fond of seeing life in all its phases, let me turn to what perhaps may be more interesting to the reader.

Among other remarkable occurrences of this time was that of three courts-martial held in succession on three distinguished officers of the naval service, all arising out of the same operations against the enemy—Lord Gambier, who had the command of the Channel fleet; Rear-Admiral Sir Eliab Harvey, Bart., commanding the inshore squadron, blockading some French line-of-battle ships and other vessels in Basque Roads, who had distinguished himself in the Battle of Trafalgar, when in command of the "Temeraire," of ninety-eight guns, engaging and taking a French and Spanish line-of-battle ship at the same time; and Captain Lord Cochrane, who was sent out by the Admiralty to take the command of some fire-ships, for the destruction of the enemy's force.

On the return of the fleet to Spithead from this successful enterprise, it was soon made public that an altercation or disagreement of an unpleasant nature had taken place between the senior officers, which was likely to lead to unpleasant consequences.

My Lord Gambier, it seems, was one of the first in command, who had sanctioned the distribution of religious tracts among the seamen of the fleet. Now, however wise and politic and morally proper this might seem to be, in all well-regulated minds, for the purpose of reforming the loose morals and dissolute habits of our sailors, it is quite certain it did not always meet with the approbation or the necessary attention of captains and officers in command, who pretty well knew what sort of stuff their men were made of.

Innovations whether good or bad are generally introduced by the few, and always looked upon with a jaundiced eye by the many, and it is possible that the majority of the profession did not or would not appreciate the solicitude Lord Gambier had for the spiritual welfare of those "who go down to the sea in ships and occupy their business in the great waters." And experience tells us 'tis a much easier task to dispel the doubts and establish the faith of a parish tea-party, than it is to evangelize a ship's company.

Nevertheless it must be admitted, either from this cause or some other, a great improvement has taken place in the general conduct of the men, both on shore and on board; and we have had undeniable proofs in the Crimea and in India, that a high religious feeling is not incompatible with personal bravery, any more than clerical instruction is with scientific acquirements in the art of war, although it may not require such religious fervour in these times, as animated the soldiers of the commonwealth, to make a vigorous and murderous onslaught successful.

This, then, was the ground of dispute; and those two gallant officers held different and opposite opinions upon a practice that one had sanctioned and the other condemned.

The report then current was, that the rear-admiral, being very much annoyed at the instructions brought on board his ship by Lord Gambier's flag-lieutenant, that the command of the squadron destined for the destruction of the enemy was to be given to Lord Cochrane, an officer of a lower grade than himself, who had been sent out from England for that purpose, made use of an expletive not usually intended for polite ears, and attaching to it a prænomen generally ascribed to over, or self-righteous people.

This unfortunately was reported to his lordship, who on his arrival in port demanded a court-martial on his second in command, which accordingly assembled on board the "Gladiator," the flag-ship of the harbour admiral: Sir Roger Curtis, then port admiral, sitting as president. The charge of disrespectful language to his superior officer, as commander-in-chief, being fully proved, this tried and gallant seaman, this brave and distinguished officer, who had served his country with so much honour from his youth up—was dismissed the service.

It gave infinite satisfaction to the Navy and to the country generally, when it was announced in the following Gazette that an order in council had restored Sir Eliab Harvey to his rank. Upon this Lord Gambier thought proper to insist upon a court-martial on himself. What the specific charges were I do not recollect, but I was present at the time and heard the sentence of the court pronounced, "Honourably acquitted," when the same flag officer who had presided at the late trial, on returning his lordship's sword, gave further proof of that amiable characteristic for which, through a long life and much service, he had been so celebrated.

Then came the trial of Lord Cochrane, arising out of the same affair, which terminated as did that upon Lord Gambier; and the excitement which so uncommon an occurrence had caused slowly and quietly evaporated.

About this time, from this and other causes, a number of naval officers would congregate in our streets, on their way to or from the Sally-port, where the different captains' gigs were constantly in attendance.

One morning five or six of them had gathered round the harbour admiral, "little Billy Hargood," as the sailors called him. Now, this excellent officer had studied the rules of Hamilton More to greater advantage than he had those of Lindley Murray; consequently his vocabulary consisted chiefly of stereotyped phrases, the one most in use being, "I'll tell you what it is," with which he invariably addressed his subordinates. I unwittingly overheard the conversation between the Admiral and Sir Peter Parker,* at that time in command of one of H. M. frigates, on the means he took to maintain discipline among his men, which he had heard through various channels.

* This gallant officer was killed in the last American war, when on shore with his men on some particular service. His handsome and manly features may be recognised in the hall of Greenwich Hospital.

Having listened with the greatest apparent attention to the Admiral's friendly admonition, which was replete with double negatives and other discordances, Sir Peter said, in turning away, and with the most perfect good understanding:—

"I tell you what it is, Admiral, I don't care nothing for none on 'em."

It was about five-and-twenty years after this, while pursuing my ordinary avocation, I was passing, at a moderate pace by a large posting-house, about eleven miles from town, when I was hailed by the ostler to pull up. I immediately did so, and looking down on the off-side, saw a gentleman apparently in the vale of years, whose weather-beaten countenance I thought I had seen before. He asked me if I could take him to a certain village through which I passed. I replied in the affirmative, and the box-seat being vacant, politely asked him if he would take it. He thanked me, and got up. We had not proceeded far before I was convinced, from some observations that fell in connection with the place of his destination, that I was not wrong in my conjecture.

My companion soon became affable and chatty, asking me many questions as to the names of the mansions we passed and their owners, the quality of the land, &c. In answer to one of these, I purposely substituted Admiral for Sir. At this he looked at me with astonishment, and sharply demanded how I knew he was an Admiral. I coolly replied that in my early life I had belonged to the same noble profession as himself; and though I had not had the honour of sailing with him, it was impossible for any one who knew anything of the service not to have known, or ever to have forgotten, so distinguished a member of it as Sir Eliab

Harvey, saying which I raised my hat from my head.

"But when and where did you ever see me?" said the Admiral, impatiently.

"Often," I said, the spirit of former days rising in my throat, and almost choking me—"often; and the last time I saw you was on board the 'Gladiator,' when you were tried by a court-martial, and—" I hesitated.

"And what, Sir?"

"And broke?"

With unruffled features, he mildly asked—

"And what was I broke for, pray?" When I repeated the very words he had made use of, he laughed aloud; while I rejoined, that no one felt greater joy than I did when he was reinstated. He reached his destination after a two hours' ride, and at parting heartily shook me by the hand, saying he had had a very pleasant journey.

Another occurrence at this time was the embarkation of that crack regiment, the 10th Hussars, for the Peninsula. His Royal Highness George Prince of Wales, their Colonel, afterwards King George the Fourth, came down to Portsmouth to witness their departure. This caused no little stir in the old town. A review of the troops in the garrison took place on Southsea Common. The Prince was there on horseback, accompanied by an eccentric baronet,* whose strange attire—a long loose plain drab coat and a slouched hat, contrasted strongly with the tight Hussar jacket and the fur cap of his royal and rotund Patron. After the review the officers of the regiment gave a grand farewell dinner at one of the hotels to their distinguished Colonel, to which the principal officers of the garrison were invited, where my friend and I had the

* Sir John Ladd.

highly-prized privilege of seeing the first gentleman in the land sitting at the head of the table, gnawing a bone like a rustic.

It was not long after this that a most awful and melancholy accident occurred, involving the death of five poor creatures. A detachment of some regiments of infantry had disembarked from Ireland, and had brought with them as much as eight or ten barrels of gunpowder, which were temporarily deposited on Point Beach. I was sitting having my hair cut in a hairdresser's shop at the bottom of the High Street, when a tremendous concussion in the air, that seemed to shake the whole fabric, roused me from my seat, and, with the operation half performed, I rushed from the back of the house to the street, when I saw men and women running in crowds to the supposed scene of some great disaster. Some cried one thing, some another; but the loudest and most general cry was, that the Custom-house had been blown up. Joining the crowd, I presently ascertained this to be wrong, which relieved my panting heart not a little; for I had a near and dear friend there, whose wife was in the crowd, and who clung to me in her panic.

Having reassured her, and walked back with her a short distance, I hastened to the scene of destruction. The powder on the beach had by some means ignited. An Irishwoman, the wife of one of the soldiers who had disembarked with the detachment, had been sitting on one of the casks, smoking a pipe, which must have been the cause of this terrible explosion. The poor creature was never after seen alive. One other was blown over the houses, and dashed against the front of the Isle of Wight Sloop "Public," which was covered with blood and brains.

In all five, as I have said, suffered; but the most remarkable part of this sad calamity was, that the soldier who stood sentinel over the powder had his musket torn from his hold, and every button from the front of his jacket, by the force of the concussion, while he remained unhurt, though stupefied for a time—such, I believe, is the uncertain effect of gunpowder.

It is not a little singular that a similar catastrophe, though not from gunpowder, of a very recent date, should be equally as remarkable. The following is extracted from the *Times*, of Sept. 12th, 1859:—

"Explosion on Board the Great Eastern.—The ruin here would have been an instructive sight for engineers to witness. It would be still better if medical men could inspect them, and solve the problem of how it can possibly have happened that men who stood round the case of the funnel when it exploded, and when tons of iron were torn up and cast about, were not only not killed on the spot, but scarcely one was unable to walk, and not one has sustained a fracture or dislocation."

Another occurrence which caused considerable excitement in the town, and which was attended with lamentable consequences, I cannot forbear relating, although at the risk of being termed a narrator of horrors.

Two French officers, who had broken their parole, hired a boat on Gosport beach, pretending they were going on board a vessel at Spithead. The waterman, who was well known to the inhabitants as a steady, hard-working man, had agreed for his fare, without the least suspicion of their character, or their dangerous enterprise. When they had reached Spithead, it is supposed he refused to proceed further at their desire;

upon which, to get possession of the boat, they rushed upon him with their knives, and after inflicting several wounds on his body, threw him overboard.

Fortunately the scuffle was not unobserved by one of the ships at anchor, whose commander immediately despatched a boat in chase, though too late to save the poor fellow's life; however, they succeeded in recapturing the wherry, and bringing the two miscreants to Portsmouth. They were taken before the magistrates, and by them committed to Winchester, for trial at the ensuing assizes, for murder. I need scarcely add they were condemned and executed.

The poor man's body was washed on shore a few days afterwards, and gave evident marks of the violent and cruel death he had met with. A handsome subscription was immediately entered into for his widow and orphans, by the principal inhabitants.

The untimely fate of the two Frenchmen caused no commiseration, and the justice of their sentence was never disputed. Doubtless they intended to cross the Channel in an open boat—a rash and daring deed of itself, and attended with considerable risk, worthy of men desirous of again joining their comrades and worshipping their idol; but they had put themselves out of the pale of international law—first by breaking their parole, and then by perpetrating a crime that made them amenable to the laws of humanity, and the country, of which their victim was a peaceful citizen.

Some little time after this one of Buonaparte's ablest and most favourite generals attempted the same bold undertaking with success; of whom more in another chapter.

CHAPTER VI.

FROM YOUTH TO MANHOOD.

Younger Sister — Pleasant Gallop — Younger Brother — Pleasant Swim—Dreadful Disaster at Sea—A Naval Ball —Self-confidence—Domestic Sorrow—New Branch of an Old Acquaintance—Career of an Officer—A Distressed Mother, her Trials and her Death—Pleasant Life—A Welcome Visitor—Sad Calamity—A Trio—Duel—Pleasant Body Companion—The Comets of 1858 and of 1811 —Description of—Astronomers.

The reader must not infer from the perusal of the preceding chapter — that I was inattentive to domestic occurrences, or that I was deficient in marking the progress, or rejoicing in the felicity, of any one member of our very happy family. My father then lived in a mansion or house he had built in the Forest—now occupied by one of our great naval commanders*—where he enjoyed the society of his neighbours and friends, and where, I need scarcely say, he kept a very good table, extending his hospitality to all around. Upon any extra display, I was generally sent for, as well to partake of some choice viands, as to participate in the hilarity of the company, or to be introduced to some of his numerous visitors. Upon one of these occasions I met with what might have been a serious accident.

The engaging manners, as well as sweet expression of countenance, of my second sister—then just growing into womanhood—had attracted the attention of a young man, who had come to settle in our parish; he was the son of a wealthy yeoman in another part of the county. After some little time he was accepted, and, upon

* Sir Charles Napier.

the first interview of the parents—which, according to the rules of society, took place at the home of the betrothed—I was sent for from Portsmouth to meet them. I received the notification, at the same time, that the merits of a haunch of venison from the neighbouring park of Stanstead was to be discussed, as well as the matrimonial arrangements, and resolved not to be absent.

From some cause—I do not recollect what—I did not ride my own horse that day; and, not being then very particular what I did ride, I accepted the offer of a nice-looking, well-bred, little bay mare, that appeared to me to have all the qualifications of a perfect hackney. I did not know her, and my friend, to whom she belonged, did not make me acquainted with any of her misgivings. He had not had her many days, nor had he backed her many times; but I must think that he suspected a very peculiar propensity she possessed; and knowing that I was not in the habit of riding very slow, he showed no compunction nor fear of any consequence in lending her to me.

Accordingly I mounted, one hot summer's day; and, as I generally took about an hour—never more—to accomplish the ten miles—often did it in less—I did not leave till about two o'clock. I had not cleared the gates, and proceeded far on the road, before I found it was more a toil than a pleasure to ride such an animal; and the perspiration commenced running down my face in great profusion, till, arriving at the top of the hill approaching the entrance to the Forest, I thought I would give her her head, as my arms ached with holding her. After a few strides she got the bit in her mouth, and away she went at full speed. It was in vain for me to pull, and as I saw no danger, the road being perfectly straight, except what might be anticipated at the termination of her frolic, I stuck fast. Now, it was full three miles through the forest to my father's house, and I faintly hoped she would become exhausted before reach- the village; but, as it happened, there were some men repairing a gulley, that conveyed the water under the road, just by the nine milestone. They had made an excavation not quite the width of the road, leaving, indeed, a way on each side. It was fruitless to pull her either to the right or left. On she went at the top of her speed—I shouting to the men when coming to the pit—and not being able to cover it, she jumped right in. The mare kept her legs, and I kept my seat; but, in jumping out of the pit, her head came in fearful collision with mine, and the concussion almost took away my senses. The excavators came to my assistance and held the mare till I had somewhat recovered myself; when, finding she was too much blown to make a similar effort, I got her, capering and dancing, and in much fear of another knock on the head, safe to my father's stables, about a mile further; and when I dismounted I found myself quite enfeebled, and my head in great pain. Instead, therefore, of sitting down to enjoy the society of my father's new guests, and to make acquaintance with my intended brother-in-law, or to partake of the smoking haunch, I was obliged to lay down. I did not recover till the next day, when the guests were all departed; and my father was extremely chagrined that I had been put upon so dangerous an animal, which he sent to its owner, with a not very pleasing message, by his groom. When I remonstrated with the owner for so unfriendly an act, seeing that I was quite free from injury he only smiled, though he was not a man as I thought to feel indifference when human life was in danger, and I had been on terms of the greatest intimacy with him. However, he quickly parted with the mare, and I had forgotten her, though not the very serious hazard she had put me to.

About three years after this I was at Portsdown Fair, where I was in the habit of meeting persons in the same business as myself. One of them, a particular friend from Southampton, and a most excellent judge of a horse, saw me in the act of purchasing a nice little bay mare. He walked away while I mounted her with the intention of riding her home. Turning her head in that direction, she set off at full gallop down the hill, kicking and plunging all the way, but getting safe into the village at the foot of the hill. I dismounted, and, upon a little further examination, recognized the identical animal that had before endangered my life. I had now become a married man; and being likely to have further claims upon me, did not choose to court danger; I therefore sent her home, and returned in a hired conveyance, not saying a word of what had happened.

In the morning a note arrived, bearing the Southampton post-mark, addressed to my wife, wherein the writer spoke of the danger her husband had witnessed. It also stated that he had found, upon inquiry, that the animal I had purchased was a most vicious and ungovernable brute; and she begged my wife to induce me to part with so dangerous a nag as soon as possible; this I did not hesitate to do.

Another movement in our domestic circle was the departure of one of my younger brothers. He, like me, had been sent to sea, and in one of our crack frigates* had sailed up the Mediterranean, where his ship had joined the expedition up the Dardanelles, under Sir John T. Duck-

* "The Sea Horse."

worth. It was on returning from thence he met with an accident that caused him to be sent home. Standing on the quarter-deck, the studding-sail haulyard-block fell from the maintop-gallant yard-arm, and, striking him on the face, gave his jib-boom a twist that never righted; and the scar, also inflicted by the blow, he carried with him to an early grave.

In consequence of this he left the service for a time; and, being still very young, was sent to a celebrated naval academy at Gosport; but an offer being made by his old captain,* who was son and brother to a peer, for him to sail in a small frigate, commanded by a young officer just posted, then fitting out at Portsmouth, I had to see him on board. Though we had already experienced the hardships and privations of a midshipman's berth, he was very loth to leave the comfort and comparative luxuries of our happy home in exchange.

* The Hon. Courtenay Boyle.

Consequently, I had some little difficulty in inducing him to join; but I eventually succeeded, and he soon became devoted to the service, and a great favourite with his captain and officers.

In the Bay of Naples this little frigate* engaged and beat off one of superior weight, belonging to the French. My brother was standing by the side of the captain when the latter was struck by a cannon ball on the shoulder, carrying away his epaulette; this my brother picked up, and, turning to his captain, saw that he was desperately wounded, and begged him to go below. This appeal was answered only by a frown—the first-lieutenant had been killed, and several of the other officers wounded; the decks were strewed with the dead and dying—so much so, that after the Frenchman had sheered off, a signal was made to a small brig in company for medical assistance.

* "The Cyane."

This was considered one of the smartest engagements during the war, and upon the arrival of the captain with his craft at Spithead, minus his right arm, he was knighted; and after his recovery appointed to a larger frigate, into which my brother accompanied him, and served out his time.

After this he sailed in the "Minden," seventy-four, when she took out Lord Moira, appointed Governor-General of India, where he gained his promotion by being chiefly instrumental with his boat's crew in rendering assistance and saving the lives of the crew and passengers on board the burning "Elphinstone," East Indiaman, then lying at Point de Galle, homeward bound.

The accident occurred by the steward's drawing some rum from a cask in the hold, which, through inadvertence, ignited. The principal part of her cargo consisting of saltpetre; it soon became beyond the power of the crew to subdue the flames; and, a signal of distress being made, boats were sent from the flagship. My brother in command of one proposed scuttling the ship, which was immediately adopted, and this fine 1200 ton ship gradually went down, giving time for all on board, including many ladies, being safely sent away in the boats—my brother remaining till the last, when, jumping from the taffrail, he succeeded, after being some time in the water, (for he was an excellent swimmer,) in reaching the nearest boat.

For this act of disinterested zeal in preserving the lives of so many of his fellow-creatures, and the cool and deliberate courage he displayed, Sir Samuel Hood—than whom no admiral in command was ever more ready to distinguish or reward merit—granted him his commission as lieutenant.

Although I spent much of my leisure with the friend I have already named, I found time to entertain some of my old acquaintances in the Navy, among whom was one who was shortly after my interview with him lost in the "Defence," seventy-four, of which ship he was lieutenant when she and the "St. George," of ninety-eight guns, were lost in the Baltic, and all hands but one boat's crew unfortunately perished.

This was one of the most serious calamities that occurred during the war, and much blame was attributed to the ministers of the Naval department, for having kept such heavily armed vessels there so late in the season, when navigation in those boisterous seas becomes doubly perilous. But the only sacrifice made to the public voice, which was loud in its denouncement of such an error in judgment, if it was not an act of palpable incapacity, was the resignation of the first lord of the Admiralty.*

At this time my friend was a lieutenant of the "Superb," seventy-four—commanded by Sir Richard G. Keats—just then returned from foreign service to be paid off. It being the time of the jubilee, when old King George entered the fiftieth anniversary of his ascending the throne of these realms, the officers gave a grand ball and supper to others of their own rank then in port. I received an invitation from my old shipmate, and was, I believe, with a few exceptions from the dockyard officials, the only civilian there.

I had dined at my friend's house at an early hour, and had acquainted him with my engagements. Accordingly I left him early, and proceeded to the Point, intending to hire a wherry to

* The Hon. Charles Yorke.

take me up the harbour, where the "Superb" lay dismantled.

On my reaching the beach—which is generally lined with boats—to my great dismay, not a wherry was to be seen—nothing but a man-of-war's gig, with six men dressed alike in blue, apparently waiting for their captain; when, by sudden impulse, without halting, I walked directly down to the boat, stepped into her, and said to the coxswain, "Pull me on board the 'Superb.'"

Not a word more was spoken; each man at his thwart poised his oar in the air. Taking my seat and the yoke lines at the same time, the bowman, with his boat-hook, instantly shoved off. Splash went the oars in the water, and in a few minutes I was alongside.

"In bow—rowed of all," said I, as the well-manned boat glided silently to the foot of the stairs, wondering at my own impudence in daring to occupy the place of some skipper, who, for aught I knew, might be raging on the beach for his boat and crew.

Not a question was breathed during this short transit; and before ascending the ship's side, I silently rewarded the men's prompt obedience with a seven-shilling piece.

My friend received me at the port-hole of the main deck; and, ascending to the quarter, where he introduced me to his brother officers, I found it hung round with flags and different devices, and canopied by a superb awning; the bulk-heads of the captain's cabin had been removed to give ample length for the *Contré* dance—quadrilles and waltzes not having yet been imported from the Continent.

The band of the Royal Marines attended; and after refreshments were handed round, dancing commenced. The deck was crowded with gallant officers, young and old, rivalling each other in their attentions to the fairer sex, of which there was an ample attendance, some of whom could boast of superior attractions, and bewitching smiles seemed joyously to reward them for years of danger and toil.

Supper was served in the ward-room, to which part of the maindeck was added. Mirth, hilarity, and good humour pervaded the seemingly entranced circle. Dancing recommenced; and I had the peculiar felicity, I remember, of leading down the belle of the party—a most splendid specimen of her sex, and also an excellent votary of Terpsichore, the wife of one of the officers. After keeping it up till morning, I returned on shore, in company with some whose acquaintance I had made, with many grateful thanks to my old friend and shipmate for my pleasurable enjoyment, of which I have a perfect recollection—not forgetting my own audacity, at the recital of which he laughed immoderately.

Poor Toby! * thou hadst as true and honest a heart as ever warmed the breast of a British sailor, and as noble a spirit. Nearly fifty years have rolled away since the awful calamity that bereft their country of so many excellent officers, and of so many hundreds of fine fellows, lost to, and bemoaned by, their families and friends, occurred; and the sad remembrance of thy, alas! premature, death is more forcibly brought to my mind by the comparatively recent bereavement of a fine, handsome, high-spirited boy. Just of the age I then was, in the heyday of youth, hopeful and joyous, following the profession of his choice, he died in the camp before

* This young and active, but short-lived, officer was named Henry Philpot, and had no affinity to the celebrated original, except in name.

Sebastopol, of cholera; cut off in the blossom of his days, surrounded by strangers—no one to whom he could impart his last farewell to those most dear to him—no one to lift his thoughts to the fountain of mercy—in the sound of cannon and in the midst of the turmoil of war was his spirit dismissed. May you both, unprepared as I fear you were, be presented at His judgment-seat by that great Mediator, who can, though spotless himself, see and commiserate our sinful condition.

It was about this time I renewed, or rather commenced, my acquaintance with the son of my old master, the D.D. I in the first chapter of this memoir alluded to, and brother-in-law to the most excellent gentleman who succeeded to the management of the Academy at Fulham, he having married the Doctor's daughter. I introduced myself to him by note, in which I spoke of my former knowledge of his family, and the respect I should ever entertain for them; and begged him to convince himself of my sincerity by partaking of my hospitality. He answered mine by a polite and complimentary note, in which he stated the pleasure he should have in acquiescing in my wishes.

Accordingly, he took the first opportunity of calling upon me. He was a fine, handsome young man, about six or seven years my senior in age, and his complexion and countenance gave sufficient evidence of his having already seen a good deal of service; and I had not known him long before his manners convinced me that he had also seen the best society. Our occasional intercourse soon ripened into a close friendship; and upon his being appointed to the "San Josef," then lying at St. Helens, and bearing the flag of Sir Charles Cotton, I went on board that splendid first-rate man-of-war, and was received by his brother officers with all that politeness and good fellowship which naval officers at that time were fond of displaying to any civilian, more particularly when introduced by one of themselves.

Not long after this he was promoted to the rank of Commander, and subsequently to that of Post-captain. He commanded a frigate on the American station, in the last war with that republic.* After acquitting himself most honourably in his profession, and distinguishing himself on several occasions, he retired at the end of the war, and lived in the neighbourhood of Plymouth. He has long since been summoned to his last account.

I frequently contemplate with retrospective pleasure my intimacy with this valuable member of the profession I was so partial to; and "through all the changing scenes of life" have cherished in my memory his friendship, and preserved to this

* Captain Robert Rowley.

day his correspondence. Through him and others I was introduced to many distinguished officers of both services. Indeed, my acquaintance became so general, that I may here boast of having entertained the heirs of earldoms and dukedoms at my table.*

Through him, too, I was introduced to a lady of title in London,† at whose house he was a frequent visitor when there. Calling with him one morning, I remember her ladyship asked us both in so pressing, yet graceful manner, to stop and dine, that we could not refuse. Her features, regular and handsome, had not yet thrown off their matronly beauty, but a deep-set and habitual melancholy fixed a gloom upon a most expressive counte-

* The late Earl of Egremont, and the present Duke of Northumberland.

† Lady Pechell.

nance, this gave a sombre charm to her otherwise engaging conversation. In her temporary absence I made some observations to my friend, who, shaking his head, said, "You will know all presently." And true enough I did; for her story took fast hold of my heart, and awakened all its sympathy. It was simply this, but told with such deep feeling and pathos—long sorrowing and disappointed hope being its chief burden—as only a mother could tell it, of whose acute and lengthened sufferings my pen would fail to give a description.

She had a son, "the only son of his mother, and she was a widow." This son entered the Navy at an early age; had reached the rank of lieutenant; was a promising young officer, and bade fair to be an ornament to his profession, as well as a comfort to a fond and doting mother, of both of which, with melancholy pride, she produced ample testimonials.

He was appointed to the "Hannibal," 74, on the West India station, and in some operations against the enemy on the Spanish Main—as that part of the American continent immediately to the south of the Isthmus was then called—was taken prisoner with his boat's crew. No tidings had since been heard of him. When the aggressive policy of the French Emperor against the Spanish Monarchy, followed by his invasion of the Peninsula, caused the Spaniards to throw off the French yoke, and make a treaty of alliance with us, it raised her hopes to the highest pitch; and she had been vainly expecting, upon every arrival from that part of the world, to embrace her son, or at least to hear some good tidings of him. But alas! year after year had flown away, and nothing authentic could be gathered from either officers or seamen who had previously known him, as to his ultimate fate. Once it was said he had been observed at work in the mines, to which it was the custom of the Spanish Government to send all persons suspected as spies; at another he was seen in the streets of Carthagena, ignominiously chained with others, under charge of an Altado. But none of these reports led to any satisfactory result; and the continued representations of our Government to the Spanish authorities were of no avail. Living in this dreadful state of suspense, not willing to believe that her son must have fallen a victim to the climate, she caught at the faintest shadow of hope at his being yet alive. Knowing from my friend my residence at the principal seaport of the kingdom, she vainly thought I could be of considerable service to her; and as I deeply sympathised with her, I readily assented to be at her command. I therefore never went to London without seeing her, and for some time corresponded with her on this melancholy subject. When the "Hannibal" arrived from the station to be paid off, I went on board, and took down the deposition* of one of the men, who declared he had seen the Lieutenant alive in the mines; but this, like other reports, could never be substantiated; and not long after, this accomplished lady went to her grave, a sorrowful and broken-hearted mother.

Thus, then, reader, did my life pass from youth to manhood — my time partly occupied in attending to a business — that not having any appearance of business, or requiring confinement, was itself a pleasure—and partly on those exciting and not irrational enjoyments that circumstances justified and indulgent parents did not disapprove. Although I had no establishment of my

* This deposition, attested by the senior officer of the "Hannibal," is still in my possession.

own, I exercised the authority of a master over every grade of dependants, both in-doors and out; indeed, I occupied such a position that one day my old captain, when he called, to express his hearty congratulations at the change of my appearance, assured me that he envied me the fairness of my prospects.

My father and his family living almost entirely in the country, a distance of ten miles, I generally spent my Sundays with them, accompanied by some friend or other, whom I drove over, and to whom my father, I knew, would gladly extend his hospitality. Upon one occasion, I remember, I felt delighted in introducing to our family circle one of my best and kindest shipmates—the Lieutenant officer of my watch* I have before spoken of, and to whom, on his return from India, I felt proud in offering

* Lieutenant Samuel Greenway.

any civility in my power, for the very kind but officer-like treatment I had ever received at his hands. His fascinating manners, and conversation, at all times interesting and agreeable, made him a great favourite with all.

It was not long after this that a calamity befell him, and for some considerable time removed him from our locality. He had married a lady of excellent family, and good personal and mental accomplishments. On being appointed to the "Plantagenet," 74, then lying in dock at Portsmouth, he took his bride on board to see the ship, when, looking down the hatchway, terrible to relate, she was seized with a sudden giddiness, fell the whole depth of the vessel from the quarter-deck to the keel, and was killed on the spot.

It may be possible to conceive, but not possible to describe, the revulsion such a sudden and awful catastrophe would cause in a heart so sensitively alive to all the tender passions and sympathies of our nature as his. The object of a long-cherished affection, which absence had only rendered more dear, was in a moment snatched away—the vows made with all the ardour of youthful love, and faithfully kept, were scarcely consummated when death dashed the reward of his constancy to the ground, and with it all his hopes of happiness in this world.

This melancholy accident caused a great sensation through the fleet, as well as in the town, and for a time deprived the Lieutenant of his senses; and though he was eventually restored, I for one thought he was never the same man afterwards. He was constantly employed, and distinguished himself as a brave and skilful officer, when first-lieutenant of the "Revolutionaire," forty-four gun frigate, in Basque Roads, under peculiar circumstances.

The "Revolutionnaire" was the inshore look-out frigate, and the captain had brought her to anchor almost within gun-shot of the French squadron, while he in the barge went to make a further reconnoissance. This was early in the morning; when, some few hours later, the boat was observed pulling towards the ship, with three or four others of the enemy in pursuit, and a large ship under sail, bearing down and firing her bow-chasers.

It was evident that the frigate was in imminent danger of being taken if she remained at anchor, and of the captain's being cut off in his boat if she did not. In this fix the first-lieutenant, knowing the sailing qualities of his ship, as well as the quality of his men, determined not to sacrifice his captain; he therefore held hard, manned tacks and sheets, jib and staysail hawl-yards, &c., a man at the hawse-hole with an axe, and everything ready alow and aloft for a start.

All kept their eyes most anxiously on the barge, which, though hotly pursued, was nearing the ship fast, while the shot from the enemy's line-of-battle ship flew through the rigging. All was silent on board—not a gun was fired; but directly the bowman in the barge hooked on, and the captain had hold of the side-ropes, the word was given—the cable was cut, the sails were sheeted home, and the wind being off shore, she turned on her heel, and gave the Frenchman what the sailors call leg-bail. All this was the work of a minute, and, as related to me by an officer on board, it had more the appearance of magic than the effect of discipline.

The captain, on his reaching the quarter-deck, thanked his first-lieutenant for his friendship, as well as the cool and deliberate conduct he had displayed;

and this extraordinary feat was spoken of throughout the Navy for years.

About this time our family circle was enlivened by the wedding of my second sister, upon which occasion I joined the new-married couple in London (my first trip there since my return from sea), and in their company visited the theatres and all the principal places of public resort in the great metropolis—not forgetting the live lions in the Tower, and the dead ones in Westminster Abbey.

In the autumn, when on a visit to one of her husband's relations, near Winchester, we attended a grand ball at St. John's House, in that city, given in honour of his Majesty's having completed the fiftieth year of his reign. Some of the military, in their full uniform, were there, and a great many of the aristocracy of the county, among the latter the heir of Dogmersfield and his youthful bride, who were quite the attraction of the evening, for a more magnificent specimen of either sex never were seen. How short-lived their happiness history has told—how blighted his fair prospects the severe moralist would record without a tear—while the more compassionate would tremble at the frailties of our nature.

It must have been shortly after this that a famous footpad, named Pitt, though better known and dreaded as "the man with the short gun," was executed in this city, for highway robbery; and on my father's going to see him in jail, at the request of the magistrates, he confessed that he had endeavoured to stop him several times on Horndean Downs, lying in wait for him in one of the clumps of firs planted at intervals near the road; but my father had always rode too fast for him, and being so often baffled, he at last fired at him, but without effect. My father was generally late in returning from Petersfield, and that evening had 800*l.* about him.

As a singular occurrence of this period of my life, I must relate one that arose from a practice then very much in vogue, but which every well-ordered mind gladly sees is becoming obsolete. I relate it principally to show upon what slight grounds, and for what unworthy purposes, two immortal souls may be put in jeopardy, and the laws of man and the commandments of God broken and despised.

Among the officers of my acquaintance in the garrison was a captain of a militia regiment, who had long been stationed at Portsmouth, of which he was also adjutant. He was a tall, fine, soldier-like looking man, and withal a thorough-bred sportsman. I had met him frequently in the field, particularly with two other friends of mine in the country, with whom he was at all times glad to associate, as they were all three favourite sons of Nimrod, and emulated each other in all the accomplishments of that celebrated hunter of the field. Indeed, such a trio, with such real love for, and thorough knowledge of, field sports, in every branch, and all so similarly endowed by nature for their enjoyments, it has not been my fortune to meet with since.

With one, who was near my own age, I was on closer terms of intimacy than I was with the others. He had an elder and an only brother, who was a beneficed clergyman in Northamptonshire. Living so wide apart, and their pursuits being as widely different, the brothers did not often meet, though there was no want of affection on either side.

On one of these rare occurrences, when stopping at the vicarage, the elder brother, as became his profession, took upon him after dinner to expatiate upon the necessity of every good member of society making himself thoroughly acquainted with the Bible, adding that he feared, from what he had heard of the sporting propensities of his brother, that he had not given up much of his time to the perusal of that holy book. The younger one sat silent and demure, seemingly impressed with the importance of the subject, as he was seriously attentive to his brother's admonitions.

When he had concluded, my friend sat some little time cogitating on the discourse he had just heard, when the parson rallied him, hoping he would not take what he had said unkind, or even deem it ill-timed.

"Not at all, brother," he said, "not at all. I was only thinking, when David went partridge-shooting, whether he had pointers or setters, and whether he used the detonaters, or common flint and steel."

The other, drawing himself up, said:—

"I did not expect, sir, you would have made a mock of what I have said."

"Neither do I, sir," retorted the brother; "I merely put a plain question, and you would oblige me by giving me as plain an answer."

"I was not aware, George," observed the parson, altering his tone, "that David ever went partridge-shooting."

"Then turn to your Bible, brother, and in the twenty-sixth chapter of the first Book of Samuel, and the twentieth verse, you will find that he did."

The evidence was conclusive in more ways than one, and the subject was seldom, if ever, renewed.

The manners of the soldier were the least polished of the three, but at the same time always unassuming and agreeable. Jovial either at the mess or the

the social board, his conversation, when on field-sports, or anything relating thereto, was highly entertaining.

I was standing under the "George" gateway, in the High Street, having just then returned with him from a run with the Hambleden hounds, early in the evening, though it was dark, and conversing on the occurrences of the day, when a female, in passing, stepped on one side, and said, calling him by name:—

"Surely you will not see a female insulted?"

Advancing a step or two into the street, he—I supposed inadvertently—said:—

"I am sure no gentleman would persist in insulting a female."

The word was sufficient, for an officer in the undress uniform of the Royal Artillery immediately addressed him, and, after a very few words, put his card into my friend's hand, and, saying that he expected to hear from him as soon as possible, turned on his heel, and walked away.

My friend, who did not seem at all flushed with this short but significant interview, which scarcely lasted a minute, took hold of my arm, and saying, "this is a pretty piece of business," walked with me to my house, about thirty yards higher up the street. Seating himself, very coolly he added,

"You must go out with me."

I looked at him with astonishment, and told him such a thing was out of the question; but he persisted, and would take no denial, on the threat of his cutting me. I tried to convince him it would be more in unison with general usage on such occasions to seek the aid of a brother officer than a civilian like myself. To this he would not listen, as his colonel was not the man to sanction the practice; but on my naming an officer of Marines whom we both knew, and who happened to pass on horseback while we were under the gateway, a note was instantly despatched to him. He then asked me to lend him or get him a pair of pistols; this I also refused, but told him where they could be procured. They were sent for and approved, and on the arrival of his friend they, much to my satisfaction, wishing me a good night, walked away together.

I felt it then to be my duty as a civilian to give information of the intention of the two interested parties to the magistrates, which I could easily have done, and that meeting would have been prevented. But how should I have stood with my naval and military acquaintance? They knowing that I, and I only, as a disinterested party, was in the secret, I could not escape detection; and my pride would not allow me to forego the honour of associating with them. Moreover, instigated by curiosity, I had a mind to see the issue. I therefore in the morning saddled my horse before daylight, and in less than half-an-hour reached the spot where the two combatants had already arrived, with their seconds, in two post-chaises—the artillery officer accompanied by a surgeon. I dismounted, and, fastening my horse to a stake in a hedge, had a view of the whole affair.

At the first shot my friend's bullet grazed his adversary's cheek, taking with it his whisker. Not satisfied with this, he insisted upon another shot, when he received my friend's charge in his side, and fell, his opponent escaping unhurt. Upon approaching him he did not speak, and his second, taking up the pistol, insisted upon revenging the death of his principal, or sharing his fate;

but to this my friend replied, he had no quarrel with him, and having fully satisfied the laws of honour he should decline his invitation; then he and his friend, supposing the wound to be mortal, thought it best to absent themselves, and, stepping into their chaise, the postilion, who had orders to proceed across the country to a post-town, on another road to London, mounted and drove off.

The wounded officer was removed from the field, and was for more than a month in a precarious state; the ball having lodged in the spine, could not be extracted. However, he got well, shortly afterwards accompanied his battalion to the Peninsula, and served during the remainder of the war with the ball in his back.

My friend, after a month's absence, returned to his regiment, and the whole affair was soon forgotten.

I shall conclude this long chapter,

with recording a description of the great comet that appeared about this time—that is, in the year 1811—which the comet of 1858 brought fresh to my mind.

Living then at Portsmouth, I used frequently — indeed most nights during the months of its appearance, that is, September and October—to walk on the Platform, now called the Saluting Battery, in company with the friend I have before spoken of, to view this strange and brilliant object. I have a perfect recollection of its appearance and position in the heavens, though I cannot state in what constellation it was first seen. It was about 30 degrees above the horizon at 9 o'clock, and, from where we viewed it, was directly over the Isle of Wight; consequently it would be a little to the westward of south. I cannot better describe it, than by comparing it, in shape and size, to a large rod. The small end denoting the nucleus or star —which was much larger than the late comet, of a deeper hue, and at a certain distance seemed confined by a band, beyond which it spread out in rays of fiery red. It seemed to lay, as it were, directly parallel with the horizon, and had not anything like the length of tail that was so remarkable in its successor, for its beautiful plume-like and far-extending luminous appearance. Still, it lit up that part of the heavens it traversed, and obscured by its brilliancy a number of stars of every degree.

Its aspect to the vulgar, who look upon such phenomena with indiscriminate wonder, was more awful than auspicious, and elicited in many, apprehensions that were allayed only by its gradual disappearance. To the astronomer it was what the last has been—a great prize; and his science was carried to its utmost extent in calculating the orbit and time of return, the diameter and length of tail of the heavenly body, the distance from the sun and our earth, as well as the rate of travelling and destination of this singular luminary; and, by a happy conjunction, it also enabled him to establish a further proof of the vaporous elements of those erratic messengers—as Arcturus, a star of the first magnitude, shone with increased brilliancy through its nucleus.

To the speculative philosopher it would display the omniscience and the will of the great Creator, in setting bounds to the human understanding, and drawing the line of demarcation between scientific proof and dubitable conjecture; sufficient to develop the infinite power and wisdom of the great Architect of the universe,—and to denote the feebleness and the failure of our faculties when attempting to penetrate beyond those limits to which His immutable law has confined them.

Thus it is that human intellect of the highest order, ever prone to apply the rules of science to things beyond its reach, becomes lost in perplexity and confounded by a sense of its own incapacity. And thus it ever will be, till that great change takes place, when the wonders and the secrets, as well as the glory, of the Deity, shall be made manifest to all those who have been true believers in, and faithful followers of, His holy Word. Therefore, as to a knowledge of animal life in either Venus or Jupiter, or of the purpose of the Almighty in creating spheres at such immeasurable distance from our planet, and solving the problem of the plurality of worlds, the ignorant peasant is on a par with the Astronomer Royal, or the first scholar in Europe.*

* When the subject lies so far beyond our reach, the difference between the highest and the lowest of human understandings may indeed be calculated as infinitely small.—Gibbon.

CHAPTER VII.

COURTSHIP.

The New Forest — The Confines of Dorset — A Country Town—Shooting—Lord Chancellor Eldon—Encombe—Sir Walter Raleigh—Smoking—Lulworth—Corfe Castle —Edward the Martyr—King John—Lady Bankes—The Heroes of the Parliamentary Army—Christian Preachers —Education—An Original Sect—A Legend—The Isle of Wight — The Royal Cockpit — A Joke — The Duke of Devonshire—Two Foreign Princes—A Prince of Coach Proprietors—Friend in Need — A False Step—An Establishment — Wedding—Breach of the Law—Mr. Justice Burroughs—Soberton Downs—An Israelite Sportsman—A Bet—A Fracas—Law-Suit—Judge Gazelee—A Dispute on a Point of Law—Mr. Serjeant Pell.

In the preceding chapters the reader will observe, that I brought the history of my life down nearly to the close of an epoch when, though the mind is generally occupied in daily business or present enjoyment, the heart is left open to impressions that turn the stream of thought to the anticipation of a more durable and a more rational felicity.

In seeking, or perhaps in finding without seeking, an object whose qualifications would lead to the realization of a very pleasing vision, I was induced seriously to consider that alteration in my condition for which I had manifested, (chiefly from the example of my associates,) a strong predisposition. This object had fixed my attention for some little time; how, or in what way, or under what circumstances, my heart received that impression, it matters not now to relate—let it suffice to say that it was commenced in melancholy, and so terminated; but having entertained an idea, I was determined to carry it out, with indefatigable perseverance, to its natural result.

This caused me many a long, but always pleasant, though solitary ride, along the glades of the New Forest, a locality full of the most picturesque landscapes, and rife with historical events. Here I beheld the smoke curling from the thatched roof of the woodman's cottage, with its garden and nicely-trimmed fence, and a solitary cow contentedly ruminating on the luxuriant lawn before it; while at irregular distances stood in their perfection some of the best specimens of the majestic oak:—there to the right of the lone public, called Stony Cross, were the remains of the tree from which glanced the arrow that lay the second William dead;—while I was admiring one or recalling the other, came bounding by, a herd of the most graceful animals in the creation, all tending to give additional zest to the pleasing romance that was uppermost in my mind.

Well mounted I passed on, I remember, through the small but clean and pleasant town of Ringwood; and, pursuing my journey westward, entered upon those dreary, and seemingly interminable heaths that connect the two counties, till I arrived at an old decayed town in Dorsetshire.

In my first journey I was quite a stranger to the country for the last twenty miles, and as I mused over the great extent of black uncultivated land which met my eye on every side, producing nothing but stunted fern, that a few half-starved sheep were browsing on, I could but contrast it with the sunny downs of Hampshire, and the wood-crowned hills of Surrey; the former affording pasture to innumerable flocks of that valuable animal, the latter testifying to the good effects arising from the judicious employment of capital and labour.

It being dark on my arrival at the principal inn, the instructions I gave the ostler, as to taking care of the good horse that had brought me more than sixty miles that day, elicited a few remarks, which I afterwards learned from some of the towns-people who had followed me into the inn yard, or issued from the house on seeing the arrival of a stranger.

"I wonders who he be?" said one.

"What be he come vor?" said another; whilst a third, who pretended to be more knowing than the others, observed:—

"I dun know who he be, or what he be come vor, but he have got a good oss, and knows how to take care on-un."

Inquiring my way to the house I wanted, I was easily directed, and, knocking at the door, met with a hearty and kind reception from all the members of the family, which then consisted of but three—who were attired in mourning for the recent loss of a beautiful and amiable elder daughter in the bloom of life. Retiring early to bed and sleeping sound, I did not wake till morning, when, my room being in front of the house, my senses were aroused by the strangest cries, which to me were quite unintelligible.

"Marn-tée," from shrill and aged female voices, was the most prevalent, and which I was duly informed at the breakfast-table was intended to convey the morning's salutation. Upon rising, the father of my intended bride, a fine handsome man, somewhat under sixty years of age, with a countenance blooming with health and expressive of good-humour, proposing a walk, we sallied out to take a view of, to me, this interesting old town.

Its decayed and overthrown walls, erected for defence against the common enemy, are now the site of productive gardens, set aside by the owner of the soil for the accommodation of the inhabitants; and they give evidence of a much larger area and a more numerous population, while the ivy-grown towers and walls of dilapidated churches afford as ample testimony of the ancients, though more remote and rude magnificence of this important possession of our Saxon ancestors.

Situated at the head of the estuary that opens its way through the harbour of Poole into the ocean, it was not difficult of access to those enterprising and bold pirates that so continually harassed our coasts; and their frequent visits to this town and neighbourhood, exemplified by many large barrows, would give reason to suppose that not only was this part of our island much more thickly populated, but that the soil was of a more productive nature than it is at present; for if it then bore the same appearance it now does, there was little to be devastated, and nothing to carry away; therefore nothing to invite the presence of the roving Viking, or to reward the courage of a conquering army, or a rival nation.

Many were the recognitions that passed between the companion of my walk and the townspeople we met; and I could but smile at the rude dialect and primitive manners and appearance of the generality of the inhabitants of this isolated district—a district, devoid as it was of that first step towards civilization, a stage-coach: for it only communicated with the world by a boy, the sound of whose horn immediately reminded me of Cowper's animated description—

"Hark, 'tis the twanging horn o'er yonder bridge!
He comes, the herald of a noisy world,
With spattered boots, strapt waist, and frozen locks,
News from all nations lumbering at his back."

During my first visit, which was necessarily short, on account of my father's business at home, I was introduced to some of the *elite* of the town, which was the means of my becoming acquainted with a few respectable families in the Isle of Purbeck, as that part of Dorsetshire is called that extends from the river Frome to the sea. Their hospitality I frequently enjoyed, and in the shooting season I was always a welcome visitor.

I remember on one occasion shooting with a gentleman whose land joined on to the Encombe estate, the property of the late Lord Chancellor Eldon, who had then recently purchased it from the family of Mr. Moreton Pitt, at which retired spot he always spent the summer vacation. Walking towards the plantation that set bounds to my companion's beat, I observed at a short distance a portly-looking gentleman, with a gun in his hand, a brace of dogs at his feet, and an attendant close by. At the moment a fine cock pheasant got up, which the gentleman fired at, but missed. The bird flying towards the plantation crossed our path, when the temptation being too strong to resist, I levelled my Manton, and the bird dropped. Upon my friend's informing me that the stranger was Lord Eldon, I ran and picked up the bird, and with a slight obeisance, begged his Lordship's acceptance of it.

"Oh, no, sir," said his Lordship—"keep the bird, I pray; 'twas a fair shot, and you are entitled to it."

So saying, he turned to my friend, and conversed with him on the growth of Swede turnips, which had only recently been cultivated in that district. He then went in at the white gate that leads down to the mansion, wishing us good morning.

In the following spring or summer, I revisited this spot with a few friends of both sexes, in a carriage, and entering by the same white gate, I found it required some little experience and care, as we drove down the steep declivity, planted on either side with thriving trees of every variety, that completely enveloped the mansion, from whose chimneys no smoke issued to tell of its whereabouts, so that we did not discern it till we were fairly in the stable-yard. Leaving our carriage and horses to the care of an attendant, after viewing the house, which was an unpretending specimen in the Grecian style of architecture, very meanly furnished, we walked through the grounds. They lay in a deep ravine, formed by two hills or heights—one of which is called St. Alban's head, properly St. Adhelm's — and are terminated by a slight iron pallisade, from base to base, which the tide constantly washes, and through which we had a full view of the British Channel.

It is indeed a most secluded spot, and seemed designed for the habitation of a recluse, or selected for the repose and relaxation of one, whose energies were required and devoted to the fulfilling the duties of the highest office in the state. Before we left, and while enjoying the social conversation that a beautiful day and pleasant company promoted, I observed with what apparent ease a French privateer might cross the Channel, land a boat's crew, and carry off the Lord Chancellor, great seal and all, from this solitary and defenceless spot.

Upon another shooting excursion in an opposite direction, where in a wild and open country the sportsman has some little difficulty to find and follow his game, I came upon the house where that great but ill-fated genius, Sir

Walter Raleigh, first introduced the custom of smoking—now so prevalent among all classes. It was a long low building, with a thatched roof. At the time I was there it was a public, as lonely as Colman's "Red Cow" on Muckslush Heath. Here my companion and I repaired for refreshment, which we partook of in the room where that celebrated scholar, courtier, warrior, historian, and philosopher, indulged in his new-discovered luxury, which he had learned from the red men of Virginia. A young rustic, as tradition goes, perceiving the smoke issuing from his mouth and nostrils, threw the contents of a flagon over him to extinguish, as he ignorantly thought, the fire that was about to consume him.

Another took me to the neighbourhood of Lulworth, and its castle—the seat of the Roman Catholic family of the Welds—is as conspicuous for its modern architecture as it is for being the presumed birth-place of one whose name figures prominently in the biography of the last Prince of Wales.*

But the object that chiefly attracts the stranger in these parts, to which I paid more than one visit, is the romantic and extensive ruins of Corfe Castle, so celebrated in different epochs of our history. Built on a knoll between two stupendous hills, it formed a strong fortress before the invention of gunpowder, commanding the passage from the coast to the interior, and, from the great extent of the ruins, must have been able to contain a numerous garrison, and to afford refuge to the inhabitants of the neighbouring towns and villages, when flying from the ravages of the piratical Danes.

It was some time the residence of our Saxon kings, and the scene of many a

* Mrs. Fitzherbert.

barbarous deed. It was here the unhappy Edward met with his untimely fate, from the hands of his cruel step-mother, Elfrida; and the arch of the gate is still standing, on the sides of which lovers now inscribe their names. The miscreant John, too, here perpetrated one of his most cruel and diabolical massacres.*

In later days, during the progress of the civil war, it was a fortress of considerable importance, and was held for the king by Lady Bankes, who has rendered her name illustrious, by the prolonged and successful defence she made against the besiegers under Sir William Erle; but on a second siege it was delivered up to the Parliamentary forces, by the treachery of one of the king's officers.

The ruins, which are not to be surpassed by any in the kingdom for their

* Twenty-two Poictevin nobles were starved to death in one of the dungeons.

romantic and picturesque appearance, are remarkable also for the singular position, in which the means used for their creation, have left different and distinct portions of their massive walls; one of which is overgrown with the largest and most luxuriant piece of ivy ever seen. They will amply repay the visitor for any trouble or expense he may be at for his easy access to them — a railroad having now for some considerable time penetrated to within four miles of this hitherto secluded portion of the Queen's dominions.

The glory of the demolition of this once magnificent pile of Saxon architecture is due to the malignant spirit that seems to have animated the Parliament, as well as their army. Had their deeds been confined to working out the civil and religious liberties of their country, and destroying every semblance of oppression and tyranny, posterity would not have had to lament the sweeping destruction of many exquisite works of art, that adorned our cathedrals and churches; effected by those redoubtable heroes, whose pious zeal converted their venerable aisles into stables, and otherwise desecrated the splendid edifices, from which ruin they have never recovered. While their pulpits, which had boasted of the pure doctrine and simple eloquence of the followers and admirers of a Parker or a Whitgift, were usurped by an ignorant preacher, with lank hair and doleful visage, bellowing, in a strong nasal twang, a jargon of confused and almost unintelligible phrases, which his deluded congregation mistook for divine inspiration; and thus became the means of substituting cant and hypocrisy for true religion, and a miserable and morose fanaticism for the kindly duties presented by the first teachers of the gospel.

The casual observer must think it

a privilege to live in an age when such absurdities are exploded, and the common sense of the people seems to have set bounds to the extravagances of self-constituted preachers; and when those only are listened to of any sect, who have at least the pretensions of education and preparation for the office of ministers of Christ.

He would probably overlook that weakness in our nature, that is now so conspicuous in the crowd who hang upon the originality of style, tinged by buffoonery; and eccentric declamation, sometimes approaching blasphemy, practised by a loud and voluble, but vain and presumptuous, popular preacher.

The enthusiast would avow, and the sceptic would admit, that men of less pretensions, and under less favourable circumstances, have, at different epochs in the history of our Church, founded sects, and "led away divers people having itching ears"; while the vulgar of every class would raise a tabernacle to his honour, and rank him with many others whose names have done no credit to the creed he professes to expound. But the sincere believer would fain hope that the effervescence, created by the novelty of his powerful preaching, will gradually subside, and that the dignity of human reason and the sanctity of pure religion may be vindicated by the convictions and examples of the more sober-thinking part of the community.

In the meantime, it may be asked, when will our countrymen cease to be worshippers of this too palpable spirit of a charlatan? Will education ever secure the mind of the multitude from the inroads or allurements of fashion and of folly, and prevent the senses being captivated by the display of gross dramatic misrepresentations, with an unhallowed colloquy, assisted only by stentorian lungs and not very graceful action?

The preaching of Irving, and the delusive mockery of the unknown tongues, may live in the recollection of some of my readers, who will not fail to compare, when recognising a similar attraction, the merits of these two religious stars. Both possessed original conceptions, or, rather, misconceptions, but the one displayed a manly eloquence, in which attainments of the highest order shone forth, and maintained a dignified attitude and graceful delivery throughout; while the other, in order to enforce his doctrine, at all times acceptable to the ignorant, and to please the fancies of his congregation, is obliged, in the absence of genius, to call in the aid of the mountebank.

It is with far different feelings we review the vestiges of the infatuation of former days, in the peculiar dress and formal manners of one particular sect, who are not on the increase, nor do they by any of the arts of proselytism seek to propagate their singular doctrines; indeed, among the principal families of this wealthy and hitherto innocuous sect, those outward marks of observance are falling into desuetude: while they themselves aim at a much higher distinction, by becoming the practical dispensers of a pure and more useful philanthropy: thus exhibiting Christianity in its brightest phase, and putting to shame the vapid denunciations of the idol of the vulgar.

If I might be allowed to dwell upon the interesting objects this part of our island contains, I could tell of a drive to Abbey Milton, then the splendid seat of the Damer or Dorchester family, since, I believe, passed to some wealthy merchant —of Bryanston, the equally magnificent mansion and domain of Mr., now Lord Portman—of Charborough, then the seat of Mr. Drax Grosvenor, remarkable chiefly, in an historical view, for its being the spot where the plan of that glorious revolution which drove James from the throne of these realms was concocted: this is duly recorded over the door of a small building in the grounds *—of Woodbury Hill, from whence the view over the surrounding country is most extensive—and of the small town of Swanage, with its long, narrow, single street, terminating in a parapet or battery, mounting about nine guns, commanding

* The following is the inscription:—"Under this roof, in the year 1686, a set of patriotic gentlemen of this place concocted the plan of the glorious revolution, with the immortal King William, to whom we owe our deliverance from popery and slavery—the expulsion of the tyrant race of the Stuarts—the restitution of our liberties—security of our property, and the establishment of our national honour and wealth. Englishmen, remember this era, and consider that your liberty, obtained by the virtue of your ancestors, must be maintained by yourselves!"

the entrance to the Needles; as well as a fine view of the beautiful island, now the resort of so many fashionable visitors, and the frequent residence of the sovereign of these kingdoms, and her youthful family, on whose welfare the hopes of the nation are fixed: and where, among the hospitable yeomen, I have spent many a rollicking day. One of my friends kept an excellent pack of harriers with which to entertain his friends in and out of the island, and it did not require a father's last will to enforce this as an obligation; another was famed for a superior breed of game-cocks, called from their plumage the yellow-legged duck-wing, and annually invited some few amateurs to witness an exhibition of their natural propensity, and afterwards to partake of his unbounded and uproarious hospitality.

But those days are past, and with

them such pastimes are fast dying out. I rejoice, with others, at the more refined amusements that have taken their place.

Yet it was one that princes and nobles participated in. I may mention that, on the occasion of the visit of the two grand dukes, brothers of the Emperor Alexander, to this country a few years later, an exhibition of this description took place at the Royal Cockpit, Westminster, for the express purpose of instructing their imperial highnesses in the amusements that were considered characteristic of us Islanders. The admission was by tickets, distributed to the members of the aristocracy then in town, and to some favoured individuals, friends of Mr. Jackson, of pugilistic celebrity, who was appointed to superintend the arrangements. I was in London at the time, without any thought of obtaining a ticket, but just on the day I accidentally met with a well-known wine-merchant, who was generally put on, as the term is, on such occasions, being on the best of terms with Mr. Jackson. He asked me to dine with him, stating that he should have to leave me early, as he had to attend at the pit at Westminster. Not being better engaged, I accepted his invitation. At the table he ventured an apology, told me the nature of his engagement, and expressed regret that he could not introduce me, tickets not being obtainable for any money, nor even by any favour — which did not fail to strengthen my desire of witnessing the scene.

Accordingly, rising after wine, he would have taken leave of me at his door, but I saying that I was going down Parliament Street, we walked together. At the corner of Bridge Street he would have left me, but I expressed a desire to see him to the entrance, for I did not know where this celebrated pit was. I did so, and taking leave of me he went in. Instead of returning, I suddenly resolved upon following him. He was a full-sized man, both in height and width, and occupied the whole passage which led to where the person who was appointed to take the tickets, sat. I observed my friend give him an authoritative nod, and, following immediately in his wake, unknown to him, did the same, and was allowed to pass without a question.

On entering the arena, I turned in an opposite direction to that which my friend took, and got an excellent place, both for a view of what was going on, as well as of the two foreign princes, who stood on each side the Duke of

Devonshire; his Grace was conspicuous for the silver trumpet he constantly applied to his ear, being, as I supposed, very deaf. The fine figures of both the illustrious visitors attracted great attention, but chiefly the form and features of the elder, who afterwards became the Emperor Nicholas.

My friend, who stood near them, in catching my eye, looked unutterable astonishment, and came round and asked me what means I had used to gain admittance—suspecting bribery, as I supposed. When I had told him the very easy way by which I had obtained my object, he could scarcely believe me, but gave me credit for tact and self-possession.

To resume the thread of my narrative: There was nothing now wanting to the consummation of all my wishes but a suitable establishment, and this circumstances seemed to favour—circumstances that appeared to me at the time to be most propitious, but which afterwards proved to be destructive of everything that could prolong the prosperity and welfare of our family.

I have stated in a former part of this work that my father had been for a short time in possession of a large concern in London, from which he had retired in favour of the former proprietor, through whose original bankruptcy he became its purchaser. This gentleman was an aspiring, ambitious man, not unlike, in looks and person, the then Prince of Wales, whose style of dress, habits, and manner he was fond of imitating; with an intellect well constituted to be at the head of an extensive and popular establishment, had he confined himself to its legitimate pursuits; but, failing this, he fell into difficulties, and was indebted to his corn-merchant a very considerable sum, at the same time was in a very declining state of health. To extricate himself from the one, and recover the other, could only be accomplished by the disposal of his very extensive concern.

The negociation for carrying out this last resource was left in the hands of the representatives of—at the same time one of the principals in—the firm to which he was so largely indebted.

This gentleman was a man of very pleasing, I may say insinuating, manners, as well as of good habits of business; there was rather a benevolent expression in his countenance, that would disarm a man of my father's calibre, from any suspicion of selfish intrigue or personal advantage—indeed, there was a straightforward, honest simplicity, as we thought, in making my parent the first offer of this extensive and, as he represented, very lucrative concern, that bore the mark of former friendship and a strong desire to serve him; and it required a man of little more penetration than he possessed, to assure himself that all this kindness of manner and condescension—for he held a high position among the merchants and bankers in the City—proceeded as much, or more, from the prospect he had of securing his debt, should my father fall in with his advice, and become the purchaser, as it did from the great desire he professed to have of advancing his fortunes.

But this is human nature, after all; and 10,000*l.* weighs heavy in the scale against the lighter commodities of probity, honour, friendship, or any other good feeling the philanthropist or true Christian may put in against it. Be this as it may, the more difficult problem to solve is, how a man in my father's position, and with his property, —which at that time amounted, in land and houses alone, to between sixty and seventy thousand pounds—and deriving as well a handsome income from a business that was no trouble to him; living in the enjoyment of every comfort, and keeping his pack of harriers; should all at once plunge into a concern that required daily application, a capacity for complications, a mind well tutored in the ways and wiles of the world, and a perfect knowledge of the tricks and chicanery which the Londoners deem so high an attainment, to manage with any degree of comfort to his mind or benefit to his interest.

In all these qualifications, except the first, perhaps, my respected parent was eminently deficient; consequently he soon became a mark for the designs of an unprincipled set of men within the coaching circle, and among them the individual whom my father's injudiciously large expenditure and liberality had set at liberty, was the first to take advantage of his want of penetration and knowledge of our species—or, to speak more plainly, of the arts and villany of mankind.

I have dwelt thus long upon the first step towards the ruin of my hitherto prosperous parent and his family; and as in the course of this narrative I shall have occasion to revert to this unhappy subject, I will merely observe that when he first entertained the offer of his professed friend, it is more than probable that a consideration for me and my prospects influenced him to accept it.

I had now arrived at the age of twenty-one, when young men look for a participation in the advantages their parents may have reaped for them, and have it in their power, without difficulty or inconvenience, to bestow. There was no necessity for my expressing a wish on this subject, for my father, anxious to enter on his new engagement, set apart a portion of the business at Portsmouth for my individual and independent support; and having already sanctioned the matrimonial connection I had formed, he advised an early settlement of it—that as his time would now be wholly taken up in London, I might devote mine to looking after his interest, as well as my own, in Hampshire; instead of spending it in taking long journeys, and rambling over the heaths, and studying the natural curiosities and antiquities of Dorsetshire.

Accordingly, a house that he had recently purchased, under peculiar circumstances, for 3000*l.*, was handsomely furnished for the reception of a new married couple, and I lost no time in making the object of my choice the mistress of a modest, though respectable abode. To witness the ceremony, I invited the friend and companion I have before spoken of, and his wife to accompany me; and my elder sister being already on a visit to the family of my intended, everything passed off without any remarkable incident, except that it was quite an event in the old town. Young maidens strewing flowers, old matrons smiling and curtseying in our path, and there were other symbols of gratulation and respect, which denoted that one, at least, was an especial favourite in the sphere in which she moved, and lived among those whose esteem she had gained, and who now mixed tears with their smiles at her departure.

A few days after my arrival at home from the wedding trip I had to appear first before the grand jury—then in court at the quarter sessions—before the Recorder of Portsmouth, afterwards Mr. Justice Burroughs, in a case of false imprisonment;

that nearly caused a rupture between me and the friend I had recently selected as my companion upon so happy an occasion.

About five or six weeks before that event, the L.S.—the society I have before spoken of—spent the evening with a member, who lived at some little distance. In returning, three of us, whose homes lay in the same direction, were walking quietly together. My friend's voice, which was at no time a falsetto, attracted the notice of the sergeant of the guard, who, with two of his men, were going the rounds; he challenged us, and demanded the countersign.

My friend, not being accustomed to obey so peremptory an order, himself commanding at the time the volunteer rifle corps, a little altercation ensued, which ended in all three of us being taken to the guard-house, where we were detained some little time; but on the arrival of the Field-officer of the day were set at liberty.

This breach of the law by the military, in interfering or imposing their authority on peaceful citizens, we were determined not to let pass unnoticed. We therefore applied to the magistrates for a summons against the sergeant, and he, on hearing our complaint, with very little deliberation committed him to the sessions for assault and false imprisonment.

On the day appointed, when we all three attended, my friend's case came on first; after hearing the evidence, which was very clear and concise, the jury found the prisoner guilty, and the Recorder sentenced him to one week's further imprisonment.

It then came to my turn, when, addressing the bench, I said that, as the prisoner had already suffered six weeks' imprisonment, and had been sentenced to another, I should beg leave to withdraw my prosecution, as my wish was certainly to punish, but not to persecute; and, as the law had been enforced, and the liberty of the subject vindicated, I was quite satisfied.

The third followed my example, and the sergeant was removed from the dock.

My friend was almost bursting with rage at what he called our pusillanimity, while I had won golden opinions from the court and Recorder. The latter, rising, complimented me very highly, saying, he had never witnessed in the whole of his legal career such an act of well-timed forbearance, expressed with such earnest and kind consideration, and begged to know my name, that he might append it to a note he should make of so praiseworthy and uncommon an occurrence.

At this my friend appeared extremely mortified, which he did not fail to express in very angry terms; but in a few days his own good sense prevailed, and the excellent understanding between us was restored, and never afterwards jeopardized.

I will conclude this diversified chapter with an occurrence of a different nature, but one that terminated before a similar tribunal.

The population among whom I resided included a greater portion of that ancient people, who are to be found in almost every nation under the sun, than any other city or town in the kingdom, London alone excepted. Whether it be that the locality affords a more favourable arena for the exercise of their peculiar virtues, or whether they possess an inherent right to administer to the wants of our soldiers and sailors on their return from abroad, and therefore choose this spot, and others like it, that they may the more readily relieve them, it is not necessary here to inquire; let it suffice to know that they formed not the least flourishing part of the community.

Among the most conspicuous of this otherwise interesting race, was one who, away from his other pursuits, would pass himself off for a sporting character, and would often intrude himself into the society of those who indulged in similar amusements. However odd it may appear for a Jew to be a lover of the turf, where the chances of accumulation are not so positive and certain as his ventures mostly are, still we have lived in a time when we have seen one of the same race sharing in and promoting to the greatest extent this national amusement.* He was a man of pleasing exterior, and of tolerably good address; his speech quite free from that accent that

* The Baron Rothschild.

mostly distinguishes the less wealthy descendants of Abraham.

He bore the same relative position to the brethren among whom he dwelt, as does the Baron to his fellows in London, and, like that Leviathan, took his pastime, not in the waters, but on that other element where the greatest quantity of food is likely to be supplied, to their ever open and widely-extended jaws.

I was riding with others, my associates, to our annual hunt races on Soberton Down—one of those spots that seems set aside by nature for the training—as well as deciding the merits—of the different animals that had to compete for the several prizes. We were joined on the road by the sporting Israelite, mounted on a good hack; and chatting, as we trotted along, about who was to be the winner in a particular race, I laid a bet with him of five pounds, that resulted in my favour. We rode home together, but not a word was said about the bet, and he joined us at a hasty-got-up dinner at the first inn we arrived at. The cloth being cleared, and the bottle going round, to which all of us did ample justice, I took occasion, from some observations that fell on the day's amusement, to hint that I had won five pounds of him, and requested, in polite terms, that he would give me the money; instead of doing so he denied the bet, and in the course of the altercation that ensued, in which I may have led him to guess at my ulterior purpose, he smiled contemptuously, and called me a smock-façed boy.

It was true I had not yet cultivated those ornaments to the visage of which he possessed an exuberant growth, though not to the extent of the great millionaire of the present day; but, believing that I had already reached to man's estate, the insinuation roused my irritability, and, jumping across the table, I insisted upon his paying me, or leaving the room. He declined to do either, as parting with his money was quite contrary to his creed, and the alternative he disputed my power to enforce. I felt that I had right on my side, and I also felt that I had the majority of the room on my side, and that he was no welcome visitor. I therefore took hold of his collar, and dragged him to the door, down stairs into the street, but not without some little trouble. When there he shewed fight, and we both rolled in the road together, and upon one or two of the others coming to see the result, he walked muttering away.

A few days after this unpleasant affair (for I never got my five pounds), I was presented with a writ, at the suit of this said Israelite, for assault and battery, in which he laid his damages at 100*l.* This gave me not the least uneasiness, as I knew that my friends would make common cause with me.

The trial came off at the next ensuing summer assizes, at Winchester, before Mr. Justice Gazelee, a Portsmouth man. We had engaged the leading counsel on the circuit. The case was called on, and the court was crowded After the usual argument by counsel on both sides, and the examination of witnesses, the judge summed up; and adverting to the trivial nature of the case, and dwelling with emphasis on the provocation given by the plaintiff's calling the defendant a smock-faced boy, his lordship told the jury, the smallest coin in the King's dominions would be sufficient remuneration. The jury, without retiring, returned a verdict, damages sixpence. I was standing in an elevated position, directly opposite the judge, and at the moment threw a sixpence on the green cloth, round which the counsellers sat, which elicited a loud laugh from the whole court. We then celebrated our victory at the "George," over an excellent dinner, at which the volubility and antics of a London waiter added amusement to our carousals.

It was full twenty years after this occurrence when, officiating on the drag on which I spent so many years of my life, that my way-bill instructed me to take up an inside passenger at Doctor's Commons. I stopped, and a middle-aged gentleman got in, making three insides; on my pulling up at the "Bull," in Bishopsgate Street, where we also booked, a lady presented herself with a child; she took the fourth seat, and when the husband, who was an outside passenger, was about to put the child in also, the gent from Doctor's Commons demurred, and said he would not allow it.

I was then appealed to, and I ventured an explanation; but all to no purpose. We were allowed to carry four insides by act of parliament, and no more; and no more would he allow.

Now, being pretty well up in acts of parliament relating to stage-coaches, with due deference I begged leave to observe that the act to which he referred expressly says, that a child in the lap under seven years of age shall not be counted as one passenger, and that such child shall not be deemed in excess.

Losing his temper at being thus contradicted on a professional point, he said:—

"You do not know who I am, sir."

"Yes, sir, I do," replied I, "and have had that honour many years. You are Mr. Serjeant Pell, and you once defended an action for me at Winchester assizes, much to my satisfaction and that of the court generally, of which you were the leading star."

"Have the goodness to shut the door, sir;" which I did, after putting in the child, a great bouncing boy, a very little under the prescribed age; then mounting the box, I drove off, leaving him to ruminate on the point of law.

On our arrival at the usual place for refreshment, I did not, as was my custom, go in and take my lunch with the other passengers, thinking it would be unpleasant to the learned Serjeant. I therefore seated myself alone in the kitchen.

I had not been there long before he entered, after inquiring for me, and observed:—

"Coachman, I find I was wrong just now, and was much too hasty in my expressions."

I begged he would say no more. I was very sorry for the inconvenience to which he was put, but he must be aware that it was quite unavoidable on my part.

He then asked:—

"Pray, what action was that you alluded to, in which you say I was counsel—I ought to remember it?"

I briefly recounted the particulars.

"Oh, I now recollect it perfectly well; and you, I suppose, were the smock-faced boy that obtained so favourable a verdict?"

I bowed assent; and here, the time being up, my meal and the colloquy ended at the same time.

Having an estate on the road, he and his family were frequent customers, and we were ever after the best of friends.

CHAPTER VIII.

PORTSMOUTH IN 1814, AND PROSPERITY.

The War—Trafalgar—Sir John Moore—Sir David Baird—Corunna—Disembarkation—Walcheren—Camp at Southsea—Embarkation—The Earl of Chatham—Sir Richard John Strachan—Prosperity of Seaport Towns—A Profitable Business—A Distinguished Military Gentleman; his Wants Supplied—A Dinner and Wine—The Bill—An Interesting Discovery—Drive to Reading and Oxford—An Agreeable Surprise—Prompt Resolve—Clouds in the Distance—The Russian Campaign—The Campaign in Germany—Peace—The Visit to Portsmouth—Insanity of the People—Prince Blucher—The Emperor Alexander—The King of Prussia—Napoleon.

At the time I commenced life—that is, when I married, and possessed an establishment of my own—the town in which I resided partook as much, or more, than any in England, of the benefits arising from a large expenditure of the public money. The war was then at its height. Though the victory of Trafalgar had all but annihilated the naval power of France, our blockading squadrons were kept in sufficient force. The channel, too, being infested with privateers, fitted out, for the most part, in the smaller ports, gave ample employment to our cruisers; while, to preserve our command in the Baltic and Mediterranean Seas,—to provide convoys for large fleets of Indiamen—and otherwise protect our commerce in every quarter of the globe,—the employment of all the means at the disposal of a great nation was required to sustain the naval superiority we had gained. Large armaments were fitted out. Troops constantly embarking and disembarking caused a sort of tidal influx and efflux of strangers, crowding the streets with naval and military uniforms.

The ill-fated Sir John Moore, I recollect, whose pensive brow indicative of all that was brave and noble, reflected the lofty intelligence of the venerable author of "Zeluco"—arrived from Sweden, whither he had been sent on a futile expedition, to recruit and refresh his army of 10,000 men, prior to his joining the British forces at Lisbon, where the famous Convention of Cintra had been lately signed. There he took the command, and marched through Portugal into Spain, where, joined by Sir David Baird, who had disembarked at Ferrol with 5,000 men from Ireland, he advanced upon Madrid. He had not proceeded far before he was compelled to retreat before a superior French army, commanded by Napoleon in person, with Marshals Soult and Ney, and the *élite* of his staff.

A battle was fought before Corunna, in which we claimed the victory. The General-in-chief was killed, and hastily interred. The second in command was severely wounded, and as hastily embarked,* as did the remains of that fine army, that had left our shores but a twelvemonth before, completely equipped, and in perfect order. What a contrast was presented to me, when, in company with my friend, I witnessed them straggling up Portsmouth streets, in a most deplorable condition; many in a state of intoxication—some with fire-arms, some without—some with nothing on their heads, others without shoes, their regimentals discoloured and torn, —they presented a true though lamentable specimen of a retreating army. How it was that two battalions of the King's German Legion marched up after them in good order, with all their equipments, and each man with a spare pair of shoes strapped on his knapsack, I never could

* Sir David Baird was borne to his lodgings in the High Street on the shoulders of his men, seated in a wine-cask, with the loss of an arm.

understand; but I remember it called forth some severe remarks on military discipline, or the want of it, from every respectable observer.

This was speedily forgotten in the preparations that were made the following Spring for the not ill-conceived, but badly executed diversion to the waters of the Scheldt, better known in history as the Walcheren expedition. A large camp was formed on Southsea Common, and battalion after battalion of regiments of the line, together with the Guards, assembled from all parts of the two kingdoms. After remaining about a month, they were embarked, one hot day in July, in flat-bottomed boats provided for the purpose, on the beach at Southsea. They went off in excellent health and spirits, amidst the cheers of a multitude of spectators, amongst whom I and my friend were not the least conspicuous, either from the observations we made on the appearance of the men, or the hearty vociferation of our cheers. Transports and men-of-war were at Spithead to receive them, and I believe a finer or a larger armament never left the shores of Britain prior to that time. In the Downs they were joined by the remainder of the expedition, under the Earl of Chatham, General Commander-in-Chief, and sailed away towards the point of their destination.

The result of that unfortunate expedition is too well known for me to dilate upon: that fine army, a great portion of which I had but a short time before almost daily visited in camp, was suffered, either from the incapacity of their general, or some egregious blunder, to become, from inactivity, the victims of the pestilential swamps of the Scheldt. When the veteran commander of the naval part of the expedition, Sir Richard J. Strachan, was asked, after the bombardment of Flushing, what he thought of their operations, he replied, in one of his coarse, off-hand speeches, in which he used to indulge, (for he was one of the old school,) and which I must not repeat — that we had covered ourselves, not with laurels, but disgrace. The expedition returned, and those of the army that were left returned but the shadows of the men who had departed but six months before, in the full glow of health and plenitude of vigour.

I have diverged thus far from the straight course of my narrative, to point out that—while the people generally were discontented at these repeated failures—while trade and commerce languished and manufacturers stood still—while the newspapers teemed with doleful prognostics of the issue of the war—and the Opposition in Parliament were loud in their denunciation of the continuance of our army in the Peninsula—the maritime towns were reaping a rich harvest, and the one in which I resided profited most of all. Here prosperity reigned triumphant—natives and foreigners — tradesmen, high and low — innkeepers and publicans—artisans of every denomination—men and women of all descriptions—from the greatest contractor down to the humblest bumboat woman, or the itinerant organ-grinder — Jews, Germans, and Gentiles, were all making money:—the reader may therefore well suppose I was not in a bad position.

The coaches of which I had become part proprietor were constantly loaded, and the monthly dividends exceeded all that was ever known on any other road, as I had afterwards the means of ascertaining. I took advantage of the large profits accruing from my business to extend its ramifications in every possible way. Constantly in the habit of purchasing horses both in London and country fairs, I was looked upon as a pretty good judge of the animal. My coaches were all well horsed, the teams well matched for pace, and I had them of all colours—grays, bays, chestnuts, roans, duns, skewballs, and blacks—and at the hour of starting they usually attracted the attention of the inhabitants both civil and military. I hunted with both the Hampshire and the Hambledon hounds, was generally well mounted, and always took care to have fast trotters to drive either in single or double harness, occasionally exhibiting in a tandem.

Thus I became well known, and was often applied to by officers in the garrison and gentlemen in the neighbourhood for a charger, a good cob, or a pair of match-horses for a carriage, and generally managed to supply their wants with satisfaction to them and credit to myself.

But this sort of business, though very

much to my taste among gentlemen, as well as to my own advantage, was not free from those losses to which a want of knowledge of the ingenuity of mankind will sometimes subject the most experienced practitioner, as the following anecdote will show:—

One fine summer's morning a gentleman called at my office, and introduced himself to me as Colonel Verity. He was a tall, military-looking man, genteelly attired in plain clothes. He said he wanted a pair of light carriage-horses to draw a phæton, and had been recommended to me as a person who was likely to supply him.

I told him I had not a pair at present that would be likely to suit. He professed to be in no immediate hurry; he was staying at Ryde with his lady, for the benefit of her health, and a fortnight hence would do.

After a little further conversation I

walked with him to my stables, and there pointed out to him a horse that I thought was about the stamp he required. He liked him very much; and asked, provided I could match him in size, figure, and colour, what the price would be.

I told him I could not exactly say, but I thought it would not be less than 150*l.*, as it might be difficult to find a match. This sum he consented to give, if he liked the other horse as well as he did this; and so we parted.

It was not long before I accomplished this part of the task—indeed, I had not to go out of the town to do so. An officer on the staff wished to purchase the horse in question, to match one he already had, but as we could not agree about price, I bought his; and then wrote to the gentleman in the Isle of Wight, to acquaint him with my success, and that the pair of horses were at my stables for his inspection and trial.

He came accordingly—I had the horses put to, and drove them with him some two or three miles; then gave him the reins, and requested he would drive them himself. He said he was quite satisfied, and would have them; he would, with my permission, take up his servant, who he had brought with him, and drive them for another half-hour. So he did, and on his return I asked him to stop dinner, as the boat did not start for Ryde till seven in the evening.

Now, my father happening to be at Northampton, and knowing my *penchant* for things a little in the superlative degree, in gastronomy above all other arts, had sent me a prime saddle of Leicester mutton; and I had invited the friend I have so often spoken of, and two others as fond of a good dinner as ourselves, to partake of it.

The gentleman sat down with us, and made himself very agreeable; and I made him as welcome as my house and well-stored wine-cellar would admit. While the wine was going round, he took occasion to exhibit a handsome gold chronometer, which two of my visitors, one a considerable silversmith in the town, the other my wife's brother, who was a good judge of such articles, pronounced to be most valuable; and of course the owner was considered to be a perfect gentleman. When the time arrived he took his departure, telling me he would come over in the morning, pay for the horses, and take them away.

He came according to his word; and as I fully expected was about to pay for the horses, instead of which he asked me if I had any objection to take a bill. I certainly thought the request rather an unusual one, but the beautiful gold chronometer was fresh in my vision, as well as the jewelled rings on his fingers, so that I did not long hesitate, but said "certainly not, provided you can give me a satisfactory reference." He having named a gentleman, the son and co-partner of an alderman of the City of London, and an old friend of our family, I readily assented.

Accordingly the bill was drawn, signed, and accepted, and the business was so far settled. I took the bill, which I carefully deposited in my cash-box, and he took the horses.

I thought nothing more of the matter till about three weeks after, when I had occasion to go to London, and, on entering my father's breakfast-parlour, found there the very gentleman I had been referred to. This incident naturally recalled the individual to my mind, and I asked him if he knew such a person as Colonel Verity.

"Yes," he said, "I do, and know him

to be one of the greatest swindlers in or out of London, and I hope you have had no transactions with him."

On my relating the circumstance, he assured me that "the bill was not worth one farthing, and said I had better get the horses back if I could."

I returned home, a day or two after this interview, and found that the plot had been blown, and that the gentleman had decamped without bidding farewell to those who had good reason to remember so accomplished an adept in his art.

The Hampshire weekly paper had been published, and the man's ingenious manner of living made known, while the very easy method in which he provided himself with a pair of handsome carriage horses, at the expense of a young coach-proprietor, was jocosely exposed; even the hospitable treatment of his gentlemanly visitor was named, as well as the chronometer and its appendages, the writers intending—good-naturedly, no doubt, for I knew pretty well where they got their information—to show up the dupe as well as the artful professor of practical economy. I took it in good part, as I did the bantering of my friend, who was not behind the rest in roasting me for my credulity.

However, the paragraph had the desired effect. Among the victims of the blandishments of this hero was a linendraper, of whom he had purchased goods to the amount of about 2*l.* 10*s.*, for which he tendered him a bill for 20*l.*, receiving the difference in cash. Two or three mornings after the issue of the paper, this person came to me with a letter he had that morning received from a young man at Reading, who had lived shopman with him, stating that a gentleman and lady had driven into the town in a phaeton and pair of bay horses, answering in every way the description given in the *Hampshire Telegraph*. Thither I was determined to proceed, offering to take the linendraper with me, free of expense, but arranging, at the same time, that if we thought it necessary to follow in pursuit beyond that place we were to share the expense.

I then had my horse put to, drove with him to Petersfield, took a second horse out of the mail stables, and arrived at Reading about dusk. After taking some refreshment, my companion proceeded to find the young man who had given him the information, while I went to call on a horse-dealer in the town, with whom I sometimes had dealings. A little to my surprise, he told me that "a Gent." had been there that morning in a phaeton with a pair of horses, wishing to sell one of them or make an exchange, but as they could not agree he had driven away, and, as he believed, taken the road to Oxford. I looked round this man's stables by candle-light, and returned to the inn, where my companion soon joined me, and corrobo-rated the information of the horse-dealer as to the route our game had gone. After a little consideration on his part, he agreed to accompany me to Oxford, to endeavour to find the thief. I ordered a chaise out to Wallingford, which we reached after the people had gone to bed; consequently, we were some time before we could get another chaise, so that we did not arrive at Oxford till between three and four o'clock in the morning. Now here, too, lived a horse-dealer, with whom I was acquainted, in that part of the city, called Holywell, I therefore ordered the boy to drive us to the King's Arms. Upon alighting, my friend, who was getting into years, was very much fatigued, and wished to go to bed, which he did. I having slept pretty well in the post-chaise, preferred sitting by the kitchen-fire, which in such houses are never suffered to go out. Rousing myself at daylight, I walked into the yard, and, going into the only stable that was open, beheld, to my agreeable surprise, my two horses.

I immediately resolved upon removing them myself to the horse-dealer's who lived over the way, and went up to the head of one of them to undo the halter, when a man in a rough great-coat, and with a very gruff voice, asked me what I was about.

I told him I was about to take the horses away, as they were my property.

"Touch them at your peril," said the man.

Nothing daunted, I proceeded to put my intention in force, when very high words ensued, and I was anticipating something like a push or a blow, when he produced a paper signed by the mayor of

Oxford, authorising him to keep possession of the said horses.

Satisfied with this I desisted, and remonstrated with the man for not telling me as much before.

"So I should," he replied, "had you not been so hasty."

I acknowledged my error, and rewarded him with half-a-crown; went in and asked him to follow me and have a glass of purl, for it was a cold morning—not that I joined him in that favourite beverage of a certain class. He locked the stable-door, and told me that the mayor, having received information of the ingenious contrivances of the pseudo-Colonel, and of his entry within his jurisdiction, had had him taken into custody; and that he was then in Oxford gaol, and would be brought up before the magistrates at eleven o'clock.

When my fellow-traveller came down to breakfast I informed him what had taken place, at which he seemed highly pleased, and after finishing our morning's meal, we repaired to the town hall. To our great disappointment, we found the prisoner had been discharged; and on making our case known, the mayor referred us to the town-clerk, to whose office we went; when that functionary plainly told us that, as our bills had yet some time to run, we could not proceed against the man either criminally or civilly. The latter I very well knew, and it appeared the rascal had made terms with the person who had caused him to be arrested, and, now the man himself entering the town-clerk's office, offered to arrange matters with me.

Saying I would have nothing to do with such a scoundrel, I walked out; and the mayor having withdrawn the officer, I took the horses away. And thus, reader, terminates this what in seafaring language would be called a long-yarn.

I was subsequently served with a writ for unlawfully taking the horses; but after the first process—of which I took no notice—I heard no more about it.

I got my horses safe home, and sold them to a gentleman in the town for 120*l.*; so I was not much the loser, while the linendraper was not so fortunate, for he never got a farthing.

It was during this brief period of my prosperity, which to look back upon appears like a fitful dream, that I frequently conferred with my friend upon its probable and speedy termination.

He would treat such thoughts not with contempt, or ridicule, or indifference, but with a tacit acknowledgment that evinced his dislike to the subject.

Victory after victory had only induced our government to make the most gigantic efforts, in concert with our allies, to complete the overthrow of the vain-glorious man, whose elevation had cost his country so heavy an expenditure of treasure and blood, and in furtherance of whose aim at universal conquest the people of Europe were called upon to sacrifice their homes, their children, and their liberties.

The disasters of his Russian campaign were crowned by the battle of Beresina, where, as one of our most eloquent English authors says—had he been the hero he vaunted himself, "on the bridge of Beresina he would have died," and not have survived the loss of those brave and numerous cohorts that his insane ambition led into the frozen regions of Northern Europe—a force that more resembled the army of a Cyrus or a Xerxes than that of a modern European power.

This decisive and ruinous conflict sealed the first act of his downfall; while, in the ensuing campaign in Germany, the battles of Lutzen and Bautzen sustained him for a time, till the issue of the well-contested field before Leipsic induced him, for his own personal safety, to enact the same bloody tragedy on the Elster he had practised before on the Beresina, which as effectually closed the second act. And now the curtain drew up for the third and last.

My friend and I read with joy the repeated accounts of the advance of the allies towards the French metropolis, and joined in the general exultation that the bold achievements of our countrymen under the great Duke, called forth, on their passing the Pyrenees, and slaking their horses' thirst in the pellucid streams of the French territory. The constant excitement that existed in our town only served to add to the inflation which had chiefly buoyed up the fortunes of its inhabitants for so many years; but as every successive account arrived of the defeat of the enemy, I could plainly see that the collapse, which I should be the first to feel, was near at hand.

At length the allies got possession of Paris. The Emperor abdicated; hostilities were suspended—the Bourbons were recalled — peace was proclaimed. When diplomacy had run its course, and settled the affairs of Europe, and the man who had set the Continent in a flame, and trod its sovereigns under his feet, had been sent off to Elba, his conquerors, to further gratify themselves and their followers, prepared to visit England.

This was the signal for such scenes in the old town as had never been before witnessed. It was soon made known that the foreign potentates, with the principal generals or commanders, would accompany the Prince Regent on a tour of inspection to this grand naval arsenal and garrison. They had already excited the gratification and curiosity of the metropolis, and were now about to transfer their august persons to be scanned and idolized by the provincials.

Every preparation was made by the authorities for the proper reception of such guests, and every means at the disposal of the more humble inhabitants were made available for the enjoyment of their London or country relatives. Consequently, not only the town, but every village and hamlet within reach, was crowded with visitors. Strangers daily poured in from all quarters. Not a bed was to be had, and such places were set aside for sleep as would not be thought of for such a purpose on ordinary occasions.

I, with some other of the inhabitants, kept open house, and, living two miles on the London road, had never any lack of customers. My wife's relatives and friends from Dorsetshire,—my own from London,—my married sister, and her husband's family,—my co-partners from Northampton and Salisbury, with their wives —both admirable and amiable specimens of their sex; my naval acquaintances—

among whom was the lieutenant officer of my watch—and last, not least, my old friend the sixth mate, who, as I have before stated, was unfortunately killed on his next voyage—all made my house their home. One of my own spare coaches, with four good horses, was at the door every morning to take us to the grand point of attraction.

The great wish of all was to see and shake hands with their Imperial and Royal Majesties, with the veteran Blucher, and the Hetman Platoff. The two former were lodged, one at the Governor's, the other at the Commissioner's House in the Dockyard; the latter at hotels; and one and all, young and old, rich and poor, were smitten with the same mania — that of following in crowds the footsteps of those august personages. So high and so far did this feeling obtain, that the epoch was ever after called "the insanity week."

The first day a review of the fleet at Spithead took place; and never before then was that anchorage so crowded—the whole space between the harbour and the Island was covered with vessels of every description, from the Royal Yacht, with her cargo of illustrious visitors, Sovereigns and Princes, down to the poor bumboat-woman's humble craft laden with her youthful family. I had taken care to engage for my party the pilot boat of the man who had so kindly, but a few years before, eased me of my four dollars, a fine cutter-rigged vessel; and had given the command to my friend the lieutenant, who manœuvred her so well, as constantly to keep us in view of all the remarkable doings of the day. On one occasion, by his superior knowledge of naval tactics, he succeeded in placing us in full view of the sovereigns, to the exclusion of another vessel, laden with officers and ladies of distinction; which elicited the praise of all around, evinced by waving of handkerchiefs and other expressions of unalloyed delight.

My friend, in spite of his independent spirit, was infected with the same desire to prove his exultation and partake of the general joy; but the old Prussian commander was his favourite object, and I need not say I agreed with him in all his sentiments. Relying on his tact and address for an interview with this brave old man, whom I had seen from the street smoking his pipe at the window, I waited outside, when, watching his opportunity, he said—

"Come along with me."

Entering the house, we ascended the staircase, and met the veteran on the landing alone. My friend, with his usual self-possession, addressed him thus briefly:—

"Monsieur, fait mois l'honneur à prenner le main d'un tel grand homme."

"Avec plaisir, monsieur," said his highness, extending his hand.

"Et mois aussi, monsieur le Marechal, si vous plait," said I.

"De tout mon cœur," replied the old soldier, and gave me a hearty shake; then with an "Allons donc," he descended the stairs with us, and taking off his hat at the foot, wished us good morning.

He was a man, I remember, about the common height, with strongly marked features, rather a prominent nose, with a quick and sparkling eye. The ravages of age had already committed vast inroads on his countenance, which, nevertheless, was still rather pleasing than otherwise.

Our company generally divided, some going off to Spithead, others to the

Dockyard, wherever the scene of attraction led them. On one occasion the Emperor Alexander went with the Duchess of Oldenburgh, his sister, to Haslar Hospital, unaccompanied by the Regent or the King of Prussia; and as some of the ladies of my company had a particular desire to see him, we took a boat and followed. From its not being generally known that he was going, the Hospital was not much crowded. I met him in one of the walks of that most efficient establishment, and, taking off my hat and bowing, he extended his right hand to me. I then introduced my wife, mother, and sisters, in French, when his Imperial Majesty was graciously pleased to hold out his royal hand to them also, which two of the Dorsetshire primitives almost devoured with kisses. His tall military figure, and his real Calmuck features, lit up with a genial smile, I have not forgotten.

In the evening there was a superb banquet at the government house, when the grand parade and the slopes of the ramparts were covered with people of both sexes and all classes.

Although gas was not then in existence, the whole place was brilliantly illuminated; and when the Prince Regent appeared on the balcony, accompanied by his Imperial and Royal guests, the scene had altogether a most magnificent appearance.

Just at the time, as if it had been previously arranged, the Duke of Wellington arrived from London, and joined the Sovereigns on the balcony. They then all drank to the welfare of the British people, when the cheers of assembled thousands greeted the princely assemblage.

I was there, and from the box of my drag had a capital sight of the proceedings, as had my friends from the roof, much to the annoyance of some of the good people on foot, who began to show unmistakable symptoms of uneasiness at my vexatious intrusion, mine being the only carriage there; therefore, having gratified ourselves with all that could be seen, I turned the leaders' heads, and, without exhibiting any irritability at the impatience of the crowd, quietly drove off.

The next and last day there was a grand review on Portsdown Hill, at which were assembled all the troops in the garrison, and for some distance round. Again were my four horses in requisition; and pulling up in front of the line, which stretched away to Nelson's monument, we had the pleasure of seeing the Sovereigns ride down.

The Prince Regent, dressed in a field-marshal's uniform, was in the centre; the Emperor on his right hand, and the King of Prussia on his left; and being consequently nearer to us, we had a good view of his melancholy countenance—a countenance that spoke but too plainly of bygone woes; and while sympathising with his troubles, we could but recall the very lenient punishment—if punishment it might be named—with which his oppressor had been visited.

"Instead of being allowed to retain the symbols of sovereignty," I said to my friend, "I would have served him as Timour did the Saracen—I would have confined him in an iron cage, and shewn him round the world as a monster." This would not have been in accordance with the spirit that afterwards evoked commiseration for the fallen hero, as he appeared to some morbid imaginations; but it would have been more strictly consistent with common sense and retributive justice.

END OF VOL. I.

R. BORN, PRINTER, GLOUCESTER STREET, REGENT'S PARK.

www.ingramcontent.com/pod-product-compliance
Lightning Source LLC
Chambersburg PA
CBHW060528030726
47498CB00004B/1116

* 9 7 8 3 3 3 7 0 1 3 6 5 3 *